Mountain
of the
Dead

by
Mike Wellins

illustrations by Colin Batty

ISBN 978-1469988597

All rights reserved. Published by
Freakybuttrue
Portland, Oregon.

Printed in the USA

www.mountainofthedead.com

The facts:

In 1959, nine Russian college students embarked on a ten-day skiing expedition into the Ural Mountains, from which they never returned. After the disappearance, an exhaustive search both by local authorities and by the then-Soviet government began. Eventually five bodies were found. All of the victims had died of exposure and were outside their tents in their underwear, with little or no winter clothing, although temperatures, even during the day, were below freezing.

Evidence discovered at their abandoned camp suggested that they had cut themselves out of their tents during the night, abandoning skis, clothing and provisions. Authorities opened a criminal inquest.

It was reported that the skin of all the recovered victims had turned orange and that their hair had turned white. Other evidence suggested that some of them might have been blinded. Evidence also suggested that some of the dead had been trying to help an injured companion before they all ultimately died of exposure.

So unnerving was the sight of these dead bodies that superstitious Russian helicopter pilots refused to transport the corpses. Later, at the funerals in their respective towns, mothers would not walk beside the caskets of their dead children.

Two weeks before the ill-fated ski trip, another group of hikers, 100 kilometers to the west, had reported seeing strange lights in the sky in the direction of what would become the skiers' location.

Two months later, the remaining bodies were found. It is believed that these four had been able to return to camp after initially leaving it. All were appropriately dressed in winter clothing. At the campsite, a flashlight was tied to a tent pole, and metal fragments of unknown origin were found. For unknown reasons, the students had again abandoned the camp. The skin of these four was also tinted orange, and their hair, like that of the first five victims, had turned white.

Unlike the first victims, the final four had all died of massive internal injuries: broken ribs, punctured organs, crushed vertebrae. One man's skull had been crushed. One of the two women on the team sustained the most internal damage, including the removal of her tongue. All nine bodies, it was reported, were slightly radioactive.

The Mansi, a tribe of indigenous people living in the vast Ural Mountains, fear the mountain where the students died. They call it Kholat Syakhl or "the mountain of the dead."

No one was ever charged with a crime. The official in-

quest listed the cause of death as an "unknown compelling force," and no further explanation has ever been given. A stone monument with the pictures of the nine sits at the mouth of the now-infamous pass.

This is a fictional telling of that story.

When you look into an abyss,
the abyss also looks into you.

--Fredrick Nietzsche

Moscow. Winter 2009.

Yuri Yudin, age 69, sits motionless in a loud, crowded jail in a sprawling suburb of the Russian capital. The holding cell is in a corner of the busy booking room. Yuri sits on one end of a bench, and two men sit at the other end, mumbling to each other. Yuri looks the part he's accused of playing: a homeless lunatic, a ranting nut job, who is one degree away from lining his two filthy hats with aluminum foil to deflect government microwaves. His long hair and beard are matted gray and brown, stained with food and grime. His clothes are also shades of brown and gray, and the driving winter has forced him to add layer upon layer of drab cloth to his bony frame. More than once someone has described Yuri as a filthy Karl Marx.

At first glance, Yuri appears to be just another garden-variety bum. But on closer inspection, if anyone cares to look, Yuri's face, under all that dirt and weathering, isn't the face of a lifelong drunkard, nor does he have the crazed look of a schizophrenic, trying to mediate the countless voices in his head. Instead, Yuri's gaze is steady and intense. It's as if he's crunching numbers in his mind or permanently concentrating with intense focus.

All around Yuri, the police and would-be arrestees put on their regular Friday night show. Technicians bicker as they try to fix a light fixture over a desk. Phones of all kinds ring and beep. Police officers, on a shift change, chat and head for home. Other officers, shivering and covered with snow, bring in a couple of handcuffed, sobbing teenagers. The cleaning woman, listening to her headphones, putters around with a filthy mop, weaving one thin swatch through the booking room. The scene is perpetual, dull chaos.

Directly across from the tiny holding cell where Yuri sits, is a large, middle-aged woman in a shabby rabbit-fur jacket. Her face is caked with cheap makeup. She is obviously drunk and berates a sergeant trying to work at a computer. The woman, crying and weeping, loudly offers a twisted and conflicting story of mistaken identities, explaining how her husband came to be arrested. The older officer is visibly tired and, having heard variations of the same story a million times before, tells the woman she'll have to wait for a hearing in the morning. He repeats his yawning response as a monotone mantra as he tries to type. When he yawns for the fifth time, the woman, without warning, slaps the officer on the side of the head.

"Don't ignore me!" She bellows. "I've been here—"
Another officer steps up behind her, grabs her neck and throws her to the floor with a thick thud. The police station erupts in a burst of excitement as people jeer and heckle, as more police swoop in and wrangle with

the fighting woman on the floor. It's a quick upbeat in a song that is played again and again, night after night. Everyone in the room is focused on the melee as three more officers subdue the kicking and screaming woman. The police and detainees alike yell and offer laughter, insults and advice.

Except for Yuri. He stares off into space. From where he is seated, he can just make out the corner of a window. Against the night sky, Yuri can see steady snow swirling around the orange glow of a distant streetlight.

Nor are the two men huddled at the other end of Yuri's bench too interested in the battle of the drunken woman and the police. Instead, they throw nervous glances at Yuri and whisper to one another.

Outside the cage, the woman is dragged kicking and screaming from the booking room. She hurls obscenities at everyone and anyone. Sergeant ElenaTrosky, a seasoned officer, bigger than the drunken woman, follows the procession of police as they try to remove the woman, who flails and grabs at chairs and desks, spilling and toppling anything she can get her hands on. The woman sees the sergeant and tries to spit on her but misses. Trosky, tired of the antics, leans in.

"Quiet, you." Sergeant Trosky punches the woman square in the face, full force. The woman's head snaps back, and she is knocked silly for a second as blood immediately pours from her nose. "Get her the hell out of here. And no bleeding on my floor," the sergeant orders.

Clapping and jeers quickly fade as the woman is taken away. The huge booking room returns to its normal din. Trosky watches the drunken woman go. She sighs. Then she spots Yuri in the holding cell. She crosses the room and leans against the cage. She rubs her big knuckles and peels off a small piece of torn skin, where her fist found the drunken woman's tooth.

"Yudin, what the hell are you doing sitting in my jail?"

Without adjusting his gaze, Yuri answers in a low tone, "You just answered your own question."

The exhausted sergeant's mood softens. She knows Yuri and has known him for a long time. She leans in and whispers to him with genuine concern. "Yuri, this isn't like it was a few years ago. The butthole of the Kremlin has tightened up again. You can't keep doing shit like that. You can't keep making demands. You're coming off as a goddamn nut. And you know what? You keep it up and they aren't going to call us and it's not going to be a simple trespass."

Yuri still doesn't move. He mumbles to the sergeant, "You don't think I know that?" Yuri leans back a little and pulls one of his hats down over his brow.

"I'm wasting my breath. I can see that. You don't give a shit what I say."

"I appreciate the advice, truly. But no, I don't give a shit what you say," Yuri mumbles.

Trosky leans against the cage, and pokes Yuri gently with her finger through the wire. "Make no mistake, Yuri Yudin. And I tell you as a friend and someone who...who sympathizes with you."

"What do you know?" Yuri growls.

"I know what I see, Yuri. Anyway, Franz is here. I called him. He's so thrilled."

Yuri scoffs and curses. He's instantly angry. "Why'd you call him? That's none of your damn business—or his! I'll take my licks! Why did you do that?"

Trosky signals an officer seated at a desk. He tosses her a set of keys.

"Because I don't need ballast like you sitting in

my fucking jail. It's a waste of space and paperwork and everything else. I don't need you sitting in here, breathing up our air. There's a whole line of real shit birds I have for that."

Yuri bends over and pulls himself into a ball on the bench. "I'm too tired. I feel sick."

Trosky unlocks the cage, and stands in the doorway. "You're not getting a shower, and you're not getting a meal. Get up. On your feet."

Like a scolded child who is being marched off to bed, Yuri drags himself to his feet and shuffles out of the booking room mumbling and grumbling. Trosky locks the cage, and they head out toward the lobby. The two tipsy men in the cell relax. The first, the younger man, shudders and talks to his new friend, an older street urchin with no teeth.

"Whew! That was disturbing. Do you know who that was?"

His friend struggles to understand. "Who...who was?"

"That guy, that old man. That's just left. That's what I was trying to tell you before. Do you know who that was?"

The second man thinks hard, but nothing comes. "Nope, don't know who he was. Looked like Marx, but Marx is dead."

"Yuri Yudin."

As if splashed with a sobering slap of cold water, the second man sits up straight. He swallows hard and whispers to himself, "Nooooooo..."

"Yep. Yuri goddamn Yudin. Phew! I don't even want to be near a guy with that kind of luck. If my wife knew that I sat next to him, actually sat next to Yuri Yudin, on the same goddamn bench"—he smacks the

11

bench to illustrate his point, and his buddy flinches—
"she'd never let me back in bed. I wouldn't be able to
touch her, ever again." Both of them unconsciously
squeeze next to each other at the far edge of the bench.

The toothless man whispers to the younger man,
"Well, you'd better not tell her then."

The first man fixates on the spot where Yuri sat
and nods his head. "Oh, I won't."

Trosky and Yuri come through double doors
into the lobby. She leads him to the property window
around the corner. The young clerk, thoroughly bored,
sits behind a small, caged window. Barely glancing
up, the clerk grabs a paper bag and pours it out on the
counter. All sorts of junk drops out. The clerk hands a
clipboard to the sergeant. Trosky releases Yuri, signs the
documents on the clipboard and hands it back.

"This one is good to go. He promises to never do
it again and to be a model citizen." Behind them, Yuri's
younger brother, Franz, stands up. A few other hapless
wives, husbands, and friends dot the long rows of plastic
seats as they wait for other lawbreakers.

Yuri's brother is in his early sixties with mussed
gray hair, obviously recently slept on. Franz is a large
man with pudgy, friendly features, but at the moment,
he doesn't look at all friendly.

Franz watches as Yuri, his older brother, examines the stuff strewn out on the counter top, seemingly
oblivious to everything else. To Franz, it's annoying. It's
frustrating. But mostly it's sad. Franz wanders over but
says nothing as Yuri systematically stuffs all his belong-
ings back into specific pockets. Half way in, Yuri scowls
at the clerk, even though the clerk has resumed texting
on his phone. Again and again, Yuri keeps moving and
re-moving stuff so that specific items go in specific

pockets.

"I thought I had a pack of raisins!" he snaps at the clerk, who simply closes the cage window.

Yuri arranges his Items carefully, a few coins, some folded articles, little trinkets, shiny pebbles, old photos, several small pocket notebooks, pens, pencils, numerous keys, buttons, tokens. It's endless. Trosky stands and watches with Franz as Yuri continues switching items from pocket to pocket, checking the weight and then switching again.

Franz talks to the Sergeant. "Hey, Elena. Sorry. Thanks for the call—I guess. Damn, I thought he was done with all this crap."

"It's fine. I feel for him. I still do. Mad bastard."

"It had been awhile, too, you know? I thought maybe he was done, finally." Franz rubs his eyes. "I guess not. Where did you pick him up?"

Elena Trosky bums a cigarette from Franz. "He set off a motion alarm in the Politburo archives. He hid in there after closing."

"That's sounds about right. Shit. Uhhhhh...So do I need to sign something or—"

Trosky waves it away. "Nah. No paperwork on this one, just a pass through. He didn't steal anything or really do anything except be in there. He said he just fell asleep behind some boxes covered with papers." They both laugh a dry laugh. "I'd say he's probably learned his lesson, but that would be stupid. He hasn't learned shit. But I told him if he keeps this up, it could get worse." She studies Yuri. "I'll say one thing for the guy, he is persistent. I wish I had that kind of energy, and I'm half his age."

"I told him. Everyone's told him. He knows. I...I just don't get it." Franz shakes hands with Elena. "Well, I know he would never thank you, Elena, but I will."

Elena heads back into the squad room. Franz zips up his coat and puts on his gloves.

"It's fine. Go home and go back to bed, Franz. And so long, Yuri. Hope I don't see you here again."

Yuri ignores Elena Trosky and mumbles to Franz as they leave, "You have no right, Franz. I'd have taken my licks."

Franz pulls the door open, and snow blows in. "Yeah, well, you're welcome," Franz says.

They cross a parking lot through several inches of new snow, as more swirls and blows above it. The neighborhood presents a landscape of endless block buildings, sheer concrete walls with tiny windows, all bathed in the monotone orange of the sodium-vapor streetlights. The deepening snow, almost mockingly, clings to every outcropping, finding the tiniest edge or fixture to perch on, mindlessly covering everything in a blanket of white.

The two brothers huddle against the cold as they cross the frozen street and head toward Franz's truck. Franz hops in, unlocks the passenger side and fires up the engine. He blasts the heat, and mops at the frost on the window. Yuri slinks in, drops into the seat, and gently pulls the door shut. Franz waits for a minute rubbing his hands together, revving the engine. Neither of them speaks. Finally Franz drops the truck into gear and drives out in to the empty street.

"Man, am I tired of you playing the same stupid-ass game."

Yuri thinks for a long moment, never taking his gaze off the window. "You could have hung up the phone. Easy as that. Just hang up."

The small truck negotiates the slick streets in the

empty Moscow suburb. They ride in silence for several blocks. Franz finally speaks. "You're my brother. That's what you do when a call comes in concerning your family. That's how it works. And you're damn lucky I wasn't in the Baltic or St. Petersburg. We're thinking of moving up there, you know. I'm getting a lot of work up there."

"Maybe you should," Yuri answers flatly.

"You could come up there and visit. Are there any good government buildings up there you could bust into?" Franz dryly chuckles to himself.

"You really weren't ever any good at sarcasm," Yuri mutters.

"And you were never any good at staying out of goddamn trouble." Franz, clearly a chain smoker, lights up another cigarette. "What were you after this time?"

Yuri looks out the window. "An envelope. In fact, *the* envelope, the *black envelope*. I met someone who's seen it. Turns out, it's probably in a different building, after all this. I need to see inside it. It's the proverbial 'smoking gun.' It was listed on one of the initial reports but then never mentioned again. But it exists, I'm sure of it, and its contents—"

"And who told you this?" Franz interrupts Yuri.

"Someone who works on the inside. I paid him, and he looked, and he thinks he knows where it is, it's in one of two places. It's been so long. They don't guard old stuff so well anymore. It gets shuffled from place to place over the years. But there's always a record, and it's in a cabinet, and someone who needs a few rubles usually sweeps up right in front of that cabinet, night after night"

The truck putters in the snow and turns onto a main road. At three in the morning, few cars are out. A couple of delivery trucks slush through the snow.

Franz wipes the windshield of condensation and shakes his head in disbelief. "And that is what you do with your pension? How do you find these people?"

Yuri, his arms tightly folded, is getting sleepy. He fights to keep his eyes open. He matter-of-factly explains his system in a mumble. "I usually stake out where I want to go, see who works there for a few weeks. Then I see who looks like they're on the cleaning crew. I figure out where they go, a bar or something. I meet up with them, maybe buy a couple of bottles, maybe a ham—"

"Forget it! I don't want to know. It's all so seedy. Did it ever occur to you that they might just be taking your money, knowing that you'll get arrested if you actually go poking around? God, you know that a pension is for a roof over your head and a bed and…and…not to bribe library…people." They drive in silence for a long stretch.

"You know I don't really think you're crazy. I never have. Hell, I stuck up for you so many times. But when you go on like this, yet again, after all these years, all those times. I don't know what else to think. What are you doing? How long has it been? I mean, you're the big brother. You're supposed to be looking after me, getting me out trouble. Not the other way around. If you—"

Franz's cell phone rings. He answers it. He talks to his wife on the phone. "Oh, hey, sorry. I didn't want to wake you. I had to come get Yuri out of lock-up, *again*. Yeah. Elena called me." Franz pauses to listen. "Where was he?" He nudges Yuri. "Where did they get you again?"

Yuri yawns and rubs his eyes. He looks out the window. "Politburo archives."

Franz tells his wife.

Yuri rolls down his window. Snow blows in. "Ugh," he mutters, "I can't breathe in here. You smoke too much."

"I don't know. Some envelope. The smoking gun, he says." Their truck comes to a sliding stop at a red light. Franz turns to Yuri. "Celeste says that it's been so long that the gun can't still be smoking."

Outside, the snowfall has thickened into trillions of thick tufts and feathers, wandering slowly to the ground. The little truck motors through the intersection then turns onto another road, the dim headlights making sharp darts in the field of swirling flakes. "Celeste also says you should come out to the boat. She's got a big dinner sitting in the fridge, a roast and potatoes. And we've got some new DVDs to—"

Franz looks over to Yuri, but the seat is empty. Yuri slipped out the moment the truck accelerated at the light. Franz stops in the middle of an intersection and steps out. He listens and looks. Only the putter of the little engine can be heard. Yuri is gone into the night.

"Well, good seeing *you*, too. Keep in touch, jack-ass!" Franz yells into the night.

Franz remembers his wife is still on the phone. "Sorry. The slick weasel slipped out at the last stoplight, I guess. I didn't even see him. He rolled down the window so I wouldn't notice when he was opening the door, clever bastard." Franz jumps in and rolls up the passenger window.

"Damn!" Franz nods in defeat. "OK, I'm about thirty minutes away, so I'm heading back. See you soon." He snaps the phone shut and drops the truck into gear. Still, he hesitates and looks into the side mirrors one last time, hoping. After a minute, Franz drives off, leaving the black, empty night to slowly fill with snow.

Over the past fifty years, Yuri has had stretches where he's worked, dated. There was almost a whole decade when he wasn't in trouble. Hell, Yuri almost married. But then, inevitably, it all came back, sometimes without warning, sometimes after a round of drinking. He'd get an idea and then disappear for days or weeks, as he went in search of some evidence. Yuri has fought a lifelong battle with the obsession that constantly pulls at him.

Yuri walks at a brisk pace. It's dark and well below freezing. He knows he must keep moving. Nights like this can easily kill an old man, no questions asked. He buttons his coat, wraps his head and face, and screws his hats down onto his head. Yuri walks along at the far edge of his neighborhood, a semi-industrial area. Vacant lots stretch into the distance, dotted by a few trucks and derelict construction equipment, all softened by the fresh layer of snow. Yuri knows it's a long walk on a very cold night. He figures he has a kilometer and a half to get to his neighborhood, where he might be able to get warm, and then another kilometer to where he lives. He figures it will take him forty minutes to cross the lots and get into an old neighborhood. He makes a straight line as he plods along, marching through huge vacant fields of broken tarmac and weeds, leaving the only tracks in the fresh snow. The sun won't rise for another three hours and would be of little help anyway.

For an hour, Yuri marches, moving his arms, trying to maintain his circulation and yet retain heat. While adjusting his coats and hats and taking sips from his water bottle, he fixates on the task at hand and tries not to think about what his brother has said.

Finally, Yuri stumbles into an old neighborhood.

For all his diligence, however, he's grown too cold and must warm himself immediately. His feet and hands are numb, and he can feel a slight lack of coordination as he plods along. He continues through a neighborhood of failed businesses, old houses and apartment blocks.

As he staggers on, he hears the out-of-place noises of heavy construction: metal tools, voices, and a jackhammer ringing and echoing into the night. Yuri rounds a corner. In the middle of the street, much to the chagrin of sleeping neighbors, the municipal gas company is working in a massive hole. The work crew is under the street, as work lights glow from the hole and light up the falling snow. Voices give instructions, and then a jackhammer fires up again. Yuri can feel the vibrations under his feet. Behind the equipment truck, a huge, powerful generator truck purrs loudly.

Knowing exactly where to go, Yuri moves behind the generator where the big engine is blowing out a thick current of hot air. The snow below the spot is melted, and Yuri stands in the blast of heat. He smiles, opens his coats, and basks in the warm air. Yuri pulls over an empty wooden packing crate and lies down on it, directly in the path of the hot air. He flexes his fingers and hands and feels almost instantly better, as the heat sends goose bumps down his neck and back.

He lies on his side and looks across the street at an old building. He studies it. It looks somehow familiar. He studies the building more closely and remembers it vaguely. Even though it looks different from what is in his memory, he recognizes the structure, the bones. He can't place it, but somewhere in his mind, it has some significance. He moves around and wags his arms, letting the warm air thaw him.

Yuri sits up straight. He recognizes the small

store on the corner of a now-dilapidated row of shops. Apparently the shop's last incarnation was as a small video store, but now it's empty. Yuri, his memory jogged, now sees the small shop clearly. The loud, warm air and the instant switch from cold to hot, makes Yuri feel loopy as his limbs tingle and come back to life. He thinks back, fifty years. He was on this very street, and he went to that shop for her.

January 1959.

A thriving block of small businesses in a Moscow suburb: a barbershop and a plumbing and hardware store. The corner building advertises fine watch repair, a pawnshop, and a jewelry store.

Yuri is 19. He is fit and handsome, and he walks with a sturdy gait. Young Yuri's boyish face burns with the cold, and his cheeks and nose are bright red, but he doesn't really feel it. He's too excited and nervous as he steps into the small watch shop.

Inside the shop, the jeweler, a tiny, thick man with a huge swoop of gray hair and wild eyebrows, fills out a slip slowly and deliberately and hands it to a waiting woman.

"Come by Thursday after lunch. I'll have it done." The woman takes the ticket.

"Thursday then. Good night, ma'am." The jeweler does a gentle bow and almost clicks the heels of his immaculately polished shoes.

"Good night," the woman says.

The bell on the door rings as the woman exits. The shop is awash in the sound of ticking clocks. Yuri looks around the store awkwardly. The Jeweler, in a tidy suit with a matching vest, checks his own watch. It's a few minutes past closing time. He sighs, but then flashes a friendly smile.

"Can I help you, young friend?"

Yuri meets the jeweler at the counter. He is sheepish. "Oh...Hello, uh...yes, I mean…Well, I'm...er… I'm thinking about getting a girl...er...a woman, a ring."

The jeweler moves briskly to a glass display case. He adjusts some items on the counter so Yuri can get the full view of his ring selection.

"Well, well, this is a big step. Good for you. We have some very nice rings over in this case."

Yuri paces and fidgets and looks around the store. He barely glances at the rings.

The jeweler picks up Yuri's indecision immediately. "Tell me," the jeweler asks, "if I'm not prying. Is this a ring for proposal of marriage?"

Yuri laughs a nervous laugh and shifts his feet. He blushes and loosens his scarf. He's suddenly too warm.

"Oh no, no, no! Well, maybe someday, but I don't know if she's that girl. We haven't even been on a date, yet. But I've known her for years...sort of. Well, I mean we've studied together for years. I...we've lived on the same street since we were...oh…I don't know. I was thinking of some type of friendship...ring?"

The jeweler is kindly and wise. He handles Yuri gently. "Well, I don't want to discourage a sale, my boy, but a ring might be a bit too...too serious?"

Yuri considers the implication of a ring. "Really? Uhhh…Oh, right. I…I guess maybe that is too much?"

22

The jeweler gently nods, glides over to another case, and takes out a little leather box. He opens it and sets it on the counter. "I have this set of beautiful combs?"

Yuri just fidgets more. It's now painfully obvious to the old man that Yuri doesn't know what he's truly looking for. The jeweler tries to help. "What about a nice fountain pen? Do you correspond a great deal? A nice writing instrument sends a certain message about how much her letters mean to—"

"No, she lives here. I don't know. She's not the fancy pen type really."

The jeweler recognizes a challenge when he sees one. He leans on the counter and studies Yuri's face. "What does she do? What does this girl...er...woman do?"

Yuri thinks and feels his face reddening. He opens his coat, trying to cool off. "Well, she's very smart. She's a mathematics student. She's...very outdoorsy. Hiking and astronomy and that sort of thing. In fact, were going on a skiing trip in a couple of weeks. She's not a girly girl. I mean, she's beautiful, but she doesn't scream when she sees a spider. You know what I mean?"

The jeweler goes through his inventory mentally. "Hmmmm. Outdoorsy. Wait! I have the perfect thing. Wait one moment." The jeweler digs in a drawer, and finally produces a tiny wrapped object. He lays it out and unfolds the red cloth. Yuri leans in. "This is very nice, and it's Swiss, from before the war. But I'm afraid I paid a lot for it, so it's a bit expensive." The jeweler unwraps a tiny precision, brass compass.

"Ohhh. That *is* nice." Yuri exclaims. "But is it—"

The jeweler cuts him off. "It's perfect. It shows you respect her mind, her adventures, but you also want her to be safe and to find her way, perhaps, back to you. Someday?" The jeweler beams at Yuri, who looks away, blushing again.

The jeweler clamps his hand on Yuri's shoulder. "Here's a little advice, which is absolutely free: Go easy, go slow, and don't come on too strong. You understand me?"

Yuri smiles and nods. He's truly grateful for the advice. "I get it. Thanks. I...I guess I got carried away with the ring idea. It was just the first thing I thought of. Er...I'll definitely take this. But how much?"

The jeweler rubs his hands together and sizes up Yuri. He likes him. He can't remember the last time he had so much fun on a sale. "How much do you have?"

Yuri goes into his pockets. "I've been saving for awhile. I've got like eighty-six rubles." Yuri shrugs, trying to look as polite as possible. He smoothes out the money.

The jeweler playfully clutches his chest. "Ooooowwww, you're killing me, my young friend. But I'm enticed by the romantic elements, as it were. Soooo, I'll do it!" The jeweler laughs and claps. "If anyone asks, you paid twice that. And I'll throw in a chain as well. But on one condition: You come back in a month's time and tell me how it turns out. Ha!" He slaps Yuri's back and laughs. Yuri grins and they shake on it.

January 28, 1959

It is early morning at the small train station in the Moscow suburb. The station is near the polytechnic school that Yuri attends. The black sky shows just a hint of dawn as morning creeps in. Fresh snow is on the ground, and the air is cold and sharp. Yuri, bundled

24

warmly and carrying his backpack and ski equipment, hustles to the train station from his dormitory a few blocks away. Other locals, thick with warm clothing, head to work in the predawn light. Yuri climbs the stairs and stands on the platform under the awning. The train sits, dark and seemingly frozen. To Yuri, the train looks as if it will never move. It looks frozen, dead, and permanently attached to the earth.

Yuri drops his bag and skis and stamps the snow off his boots. He blows his nose. He feels the uneasy sensation of a cold coming on. He blows his nose again. He's sure of it. He's coming down with something. It's taken root in his throat. He coughs hard and blows his nose again. He can't deny it; his head is starting to feel tight. He curses his luck.

A small truck pulls up to the station. A young man and woman climb out. Yuri spots them. He straightens up and wipes his nose. It's her, Lyudmila. Yuri can't help but smile to himself when he sees her, and he can't help the butterflies in his stomach as he watches her. Lyudmila is tall and fit, with two long, blonde braids and twinkling blue eyes. She wears earmuffs, and her cheeks and nose are already red from the cold. Nick is Lyudmila's neighbor. He's a fellow student and friend of Yuri's as well. Nick is good-natured, a bit of prankster and a wiseass.

Nick's uncle is driving the truck and calls to them as they head toward the platform. "OK, kids. You have fun. Stay warm. I know your aunt is upset, but she'll get over it. Send us a wire when you get back to Vizhai." The two students shoulder their bags and wave as they walk off.

"Thank you, Mr. Dresnek. We will."

"So long, uncle. Don't forget to feed the dogs."

Lyudmila spots Yuri on the platform. She smiles, and her smile makes his stomach flutter even more.

"Hello, Yuri!"

Yuri greets them. "You guys are early, too. How are you, Nick?"

Nick drops his stuff and heads into the train station. "Good to see you, Yudin. I didn't get a ticket yet. I'll be right back."

Yuri and Lyudmila stand alone on the platform. Yuri is nervous, knowing what he's about to do, but he does his best to conceal it.

Lyudmila looks around. "Where is Alex? He said he would be first and bring some hot tea."

Yuri looks around, trying to act casual. He stifles a cough. "We'll be here all day if we wait for him. He's always last. Well, actually it's between him and Doroshenko. It's like a snail race."

Outside the station, Igor Dyatlov trots across the parking lot. He carries a large bag with skis and poles attached. He walks in a cocky fashion, always keenly aware that someone might be watching him. Igor is a short, wiry young man. He is dressed in almost military fashion with his thick pants tucked into his boots. Dyatlov's tiny head sticks out of his fur collar. His round face is flat and unappealing, and his small, darting eyes add nothing to his look. He's a humorless-looking fellow, and he likes it that way.

Igor Dyatlov is the organizer of the ski trip and the leader of the group's outdoor club. He takes off his hat and gloves and walks across an adjacent platform. He spots Lyudmila and Yuri across the small terminal, and watches them, unobserved. He steps behind a pillar and studies the two. Lyudmila and Yuri stand alone, moving in place, trying to stay warm.

"I'll tell you what," Yuri says, "I'm all for doing this, you know, seeing what we're made of, improving our character and all that. Or we could ditch the rest, switch trains, and go eat fancy cheeses in Paris."

Lyudmila gives Yuri a friendly elbow in the side. "Yuri, you're so funny. Remember when you told that joke and got kicked out of primary math?"

Yuri is surprised that she remembers something about him from so long ago. He laughs. "My mother didn't think it was that funny. Boy, did I get a whipping. I remember when we took swimming together and that woman with the orange hair was screaming at us."

Lyudmila laughs in amazement. "Oh my God, I completely forgot about her! What an amazing memory you have!"

"Memory nothing. I had nightmares about that woman for years!" Yuri pulls a face and does a raspy imitation of the woman. "Backstroke, children, backstroke! Switch now, children. Butterfly! Butterfly!!!" They both laugh, but Yuri starts to cough and turns away.

"Yuri, you should come over for dinner sometime. Papa always wants to see my friends, and he's always liked you."

Yuri tries to remain calm but does cart wheels in his brain. "Oh, that would be great. Definitely. Of course. Just say when."

I'll set it up. He'll be delighted."

They stand in silence. Yuri is dying a thousand deaths. The moment is begging for him to act. Clumsily he reaches into his pocket.

"Oh, that reminds me, I…I…er…Here. I…I got you something. It's not anything, really. I just saw it, and thought of you…I guess. But don't spread it around. I didn't get anyone else anything."

"What? What do you mean? You—" Lyudmila is stunned.

"It's nothing. But you know, we're out there in the wilderness with Attila the Hun driving us. Who knows? It's just a…you know…we're from the same street. We have to look out for each other."

Yuri has imagined this moment a thousand times in his mind since buying the compass. He has planned to gracefully drape the compass and the chain over his hand, but his hands are now shaking so, that he instead just drops the red cloth into her hand. Lyudmila smiles and throws Yuri a is-this-a-joke? glance. She gingerly unfolds the cloth and is truly stunned.

"Yuri. Oh my God, Yuri. Where did you get this? It's…It's beautiful."

Yuri is washed in relief. He tries to play it down. "Ah, it's really no big deal. Now, you'll always be able to find your way back—you know—home."

She studies it for a long time. She moves closer to him and talks to him a quiet voice. "Yuri, this is the most thoughtful thing anyone has ever given—"

Igor Dyatlov stomps up to them.

"Hey, you two, what's all the whispering? What is this, nursery school? Hey, Yudin."

Lyudmila throws Yuri an apologetic glance and puts the compass in her coat pocket.

"Morning, Dyatlov. I'd have thought you'd be the first one here," Lyudmila says.

"Morning, Dyatlov. Good to—"

Dyatlov interrupts Yuri. "Yeah, I was here earlier, but then I wanted to go run some laps at the gym since we're going to be cooped up on that train all day, so I zipped over there."

Yuri coughs pretty hard and can feel his nose

running. He pulls out his handkerchief and blows his nose.

Suddenly, the train jolts to life. The lights flicker on, and after a few seconds the hum of the system chugs along.

"Whoa, Yudin, that doesn't sound too good. What's all that?"

Yuri pockets his handkerchief and picks up his bags, moving toward the train. "I'm fine. Just getting over a little cold. Actually, we were in the middle of a conversation, so—"

"Don't sweat it, Yudin. Hey, look who's here!" Dyatlov spots three other young men walking over, carrying bags and skis. Lyudmila grabs Yuri's hand and gives it a firm squeeze as Dyatlov greets the newcomers.

Lyudmila whispers in Yuri's ear, and he cannot help but delight in the feeling of her warm breath on his neck. "Yuri, truly, this is a wonderful gift. Thank you. I will cherish it."

Yuri is beside himself and turns to Lyudmila. "It's—"

"Morning all! " Rusty, tall, lean, handsome, with a thin moustache, playfully sneaks up behind Yuri, gives him a bear hug, and lifts him off his feet. Rusty is smart, energetic, and levelheaded. He and Nick join another classmate, Georgi. Yuri shakes hands with Georgi, whom he's known almost as long as he's known Lyudmila.

"Hey, how are you, Georgi?" Yuri asks. "How're you guys feeling, Rusty, Nick? Ready for another Dyatlov abuse session?"

Rusty laughs as he and Georgi situate their packs. "Pft! That guy? Please. He can't even make me sweat."

Dyatlov drags his bag and tent up to the doors of

the train.

"I heard that," Dyatlov says. Rusty laughs.

"Oh—and I saw Lexy, Zina, and Alex coming in," Georgi adds.

Alex, Lexy, and Zina, the second woman of the group, walk through the station. Everyone shakes hands.

"Well, that's the lot of us then. Can't believe you guys actually made it," Dyatlov says.

"Oh, please." Zina, a young woman with dark hair and a smooth complexion, pulls out a cardboard box. "Look! My mother made some latkes."

Tall Alex seems less exuberant than the rest. He loves the challenge and the adventure, but this trip has come up too quickly, and he's behind in his studies. As he sees the genuine excitement in his teammates, however, he can't help but become part of the festive mood. He smiles and pulls off his hat, revealing a receding head of black hair, which crowns his angled face. He wears a neat moustache, and he smiles big. He carries himself with a calm authority.

The doors of the train finally open with a mechanical clank.

"Morning. Did I hear someone say latkes?" Lexy asks.

"And I've got some hot tea, too, as promised," Alex adds.

"I've got coffee also," Georgi says.

The group paws at the box of latkes, but Zina playfully pulls it away.

"No! Stop! Not until we're on the train. And I think I've only got eight, so the last two on the train get a cardboard box. Go!"

They all scramble through the rear doors at the back to the train, laughing and yelling.

"No pushing. That's cheating!"

"I want a window!"

"C'mon, pal, move!"

Inside, the group wrestles through the aisle as they stow their gear in the overhead netting.

Zina watches out the window as their last comrade, Doroshenko walks onto the platform. "Poor Doroshenko, he's definitely going hungry!"

From across the platform, Doroshenko sees them on board already and runs for the train. "Hey! Wait up!" He calls.

Together they are a group of vibrant, healthy young people. Alex is the oldest, but fits right into the group.

Doroshenko hops on just as the doors start to close. The train starts to roll as they grab at Zina's breakfast treats.

"Take it easy. I was kidding. There's plenty for everyone. I'm loaded!"

Lexy stuffs his mouth and pours a steaming cup of tea from a thermos. "Hey Lyudy, Yuri, how's everyone this morning?"

Lyudmila pulls off her hat, unbuttons her thick coat, and settles in. "I'm good. Yuri's chopping wood, however."

Yuri objects. "I'm fine, really. Nothing a few of Zina's mom's latkes can't fix!"

Everyone talks and laughs as the whistle blows and the train pulls out of the station. The group of friends ribs Doroshenko.

"Hey! Doroshenko! What took you so long?"

"Last but least."

"Pulling up the rear."

"We almost split your breakfast, buddy!"

Doroshenko stows his bag and ski equipment,

fishes a latke out of the box, and sits down to eat. He's the model of composure and acts bored with the playful ribbing.

"I do have a first name, you know," Doroshenko mutters through a mouthful of food.

Nick laughs and reminds him of the club rules. "Yeah, and it's the same as Yuri's. He joined the club first, so he's Yuri and you're Doroshenko, Doroshenko."

"It's true," Lexy adds. "No one calls me Lexy except you guys. Everyone outside this insane group calls me Alex."

The other Alex speaks up. "But there was already an Alex in this elite club—namely me—so you got Lexy. First come, first served, friend. Sorry. It's a constant in the universe."

Doroshenko puts his feet up on the seat and sips his tea.

"OK, that's fine, but I should get to pick my own nickname."

Yuri takes off his coat and wipes his nose. "No one can ever pick his own nickname. Are you crazy?!?" Yuri says.

Dyatlov is removed from the conversation and sits across the aisle from the group. He waves away the offer of a cup of coffee. He's uncomfortable and annoyed that he isn't the center of the conversation.

Alex agrees with Yuri on proper nickname etiquette. "No way. You can never pick your own nickname," Alex says. "Anyone who picks his own nickname is a complete louse. Take my half-wit brother. He calls himself—"

Dyatlov is annoyed with the whole discussion and interrupts. "Hey, Alex, how many push-ups you doing these days?"

Alex is a little thrown but humors Dyatlov. "Uh…you know, Dyatlov, I've been swimming so much. I don't do many anymore."

"That's too bad. I did three hundred this morning. Every morning, actually." Dyatlov either doesn't notice or doesn't care that he's turned the mood from festive to awkward.

"Great, Dyatlov. Good work. You're as fit as a fiddle." Alex says.

Nick toys with Dyatlov. "Hey, Dyatlov, you can kill your muscles from overuse. You know that, right?"

"Yeah, right," Dyatlov scoffs.

"No, it's true. You can make your muscles burn more energy than they can consume."

Everyone grins at the little tug they're giving Dyatlov. Dyatlov is headstrong but not too smart. And he's remarkably gullible.

Alex, a pre-med student, sips his tea. He confirms the story. "It's true. I read a case study of a guy in prison who did so many deep-knee bends that his thigh muscles died and they had to cut his legs off."

Dyatlov grows a little worried. "Really?"

"Absolutely. The muscles weren't getting enough oxygen, and he killed them, can't walk around with dead tissue in your legs, chop, chop." Alex casually says.

"Really? You can kill your muscles?" Dyatlov is truly concerned.

"Yep. I think the stupid bastard did like 2,500 deep-knee bends daily."

Dyatlov considers it. Everyone else throws subtle grins to each other. Dyatlov is genuinely concerned.

"Wow, that's a lot. So if I stayed under, say, 500, you think I'd be ok?"

Alex drinks the last of his tea. He taunts Dyatlov

as he thinks. Finally he answers, "I suppose."

"Whewww, that was close." Dyatlov relaxes back into his seat.

Everyone laughs uncomfortably. Dyatlov truly seems to have squeezed out his sense of humor doing push-ups.

Nick tries to break the awkward moment. "Hey, Dyatlov, here. Have the last of Zina's mom's delicious latkes."

Dyatlov rudely waves the last latke away. "No, I said. I already ate. Three meals a day. No snacks.

Dyatlov spots a group of Soviet soldiers as they enter the front of the almost empty car and drop into seats. "Hey, look at that. Soldiers!" Dyatlov abruptly hops up and goes to the front of the car to talk to the soldiers. Dyatlov formally introduces himself, shaking each man's hand. The soldiers are a bit reserved at Dyatlov's eagerness and wonder what his angle is. From the rear of the car, the group of friends watches the strange interaction.

"Can someone tell me why he is even in college? He should just join up with those guys. That's all he wants."

"Yeah, he could be part of the push-up squad." They all chuckle.

Lexy is baffled at Dyatlov. "You know, I've known Dyatlov since primary school. He was always competitive and always comes on so strong. I think a lot of that came from being pretty small. But he used to be fun, and he used to be playful. The past few years, he's become so…intense."

Everyone is settling in for the long ride. Georgi stretches out over several seats. "OK, well, you people just keep on talking. I'm going to lie here and close my eyes. But don't worry. I am still listening, and I'm thinking deeply about all your insights, even though I don't respond."

"You'd better hope Dyatlov doesn't catch you sleeping. He'll never let you forget it," Nick reminds Georgi.

"Nick, what on earth are you talking about?" Zina pours more tea. She's perplexed.

A few of the men who've known Dyatlov laugh to themselves. The others' don't understand, so Nick explains. "That's right. Not all of you have been on an overnighter with Dyatlov yet. He's weird about sleep. When I was a freshman, I roomed with Dyatlov. He hates sleep and even tried to wean himself off it."

"You've got to be kidding." Lyudmila almost laughs tea out her nose.

"That's our boy," Alex giggles to himself.

Lexy can't believe it. "That is hilarious. How in the hell do you wean yourself off of sleep?"

"I don't know, but he even used a graph." Nick tries to keep it together but erupts in laughter. They all laugh and giggle. Dyatlov is too involved in his conversation with the soldiers to notice.

"He'll deliberately wake anyone napping at anytime. He thinks it's a colossal waste of time. He hates it." They all roar with laughter.

Georgi smiles with his eyes shut and fakes snoring noises.

"Yeah," Nick continues. "More precious time he could spend doing deep-knee bends or tossing around a medicine ball."

Again they all laugh. They're having a good time as the train leaves the Moscow suburbs.

The train heads north as the sun briefly shines

through towering gray clouds. As the day wears on, the train makes numerous stops. An endless line of riders gets on and gets off. After lunch, the train forges northward into the snow-covered hills and mountains. Everyone on board has settled in. Georgi really sleeps. Others study. A few play cards. Dyatlov remains at the other end of the car, singing and talking with the soldiers as if he's one of the men.

Nick and Rusty chat.

"I don't know," says Nick, "I thought I'd be a teacher, but everything has changed since Sputnik."

"I know," says Rusty. "That's the future, and that's where I want to be—on that cusp. Who knows what that beeping ball will bring, but I want in. I might even change my major to mechanical engineering."

Alex is playing cards with Lexy and Zina. Zina barely pays attention and instead chews on a stubborn fingernail. Lexy is focused and hunched over his cards.

Alex makes a final arrangement of his cards and throws down a stack. "Let me see…Gin! 45, 55, 85, 105 to me."

Lexy drops his cards in defeat. "Damn, I'm glad we're not playing for money. You're a med student. Hell, you should be in mathematics with Lyudy."

"Just deal," Alex says.

Rusty turns his attention back to Dyatlov who still sits with his new soldier friends. "Can you believe Dyatlov. He's been talking with those guys for hours."

"What is the story with that guy? He sure does have a hard-on for the military. He *should* just join up," Doroshenko decides.

"Yeah, the government would love him and his push-ups and sit-ups. He's a perfect little soldier," Zina agrees.

Nick nods. He knows the true story. "That's the problem. His father defended Stalingrad and won't let his son have anything to do with the military."

"Dyatlov? I'm surprised he doesn't just go do it anyway. The Igor Dyatlov I've always known does whatever the hell he wants," Rusty says.

Nick takes a serious tone. "You ever meet Dyatlov's Father? Little Igor Dyatlov may be gullible, but he's still a little smart, and he's definitely smart enough to know that his dad would beat him so bad that he would be unfit for service."

Lyudmila looks up from her book. "Are you serious?" She asks.

Nick nods. "Absolutely. They had it out about something in the dorm once. I was in the study hall around the corner. There was a brief argument—raised voices—and then I heard a 'smack.' Then silence." Nick claps his hands together. "Dyatlov's Dad left, and I went in. Dyatlov was out on the floor, unconscious. His mouth and nose were covered with blood. One punch and he'd knocked sonny boy out."

Zina studies Dyatlov talking with the soldiers. She shudders.

"My God, that explains—plenty," Zina says. "Wow, it's like a Greek tragedy. He wants to be like his father, and his father won't have it."

"But I think Dyatlov isn't about to give up," Nick whispers.

Yuri is feeling worse but is trying to keep up a good front. "Why, what do you mean?" Yuri asks.

"Pretty obvious—KGB, intelligence, that stuff, military without the uniform. It's all about secrets—and one easily kept from dear old dad."

The students are all proud to be Russians, but

they are all admittedly too liberal to ever condone or openly support the darker side of their government. They can't imagine any of their friends ever willingly being part of the KGB or the intelligence community.

"Don't be surprised. He already thinks he works with the KGB, the little protégé," Rusty says.

Yuri doesn't believe it. "Come on. He's obnoxious, but he's not that bad, is he?"

Rusty leans in. "I don't know. My aunt lives right beside the KGB headquarters in midtown, and I've seen Dyatlov there plenty."

The group is shocked.

"Doing what?" Doroshenko asks.

Rusty looks to see that Dyatlov is still involved in his conversation. "That's just it. He just hangs around. He takes out the trash, gets them coffee, washes cars and stuff."

Lyudmila shakes her head. "Really? That surprises me."

"Not me. That guy loves being told what to do," Doroshenko adds.

They all observe Dyatlov as he talks with the soldiers, who look at a map, discussing a great battle or something.

"What does his father want him to do then?" Zina asks.

"Believe it or not, his dad's an artist now, works for a magazine," Nick answers.

"Geez, poor screwed up Dyatlov," Zina says.

"Yep. And he's leading our trip," Alex quips.

"Well, say what you will. He's still an excellent skier and outdoorsman." Yuri says.

Nick is still apprehensive. "I guess. But as soon as *we're* required to do sits-ups or push-ups, I'm out of here. All this skiing is enough of a workout for me. And no messing with sleep, either!"

"Yeah, me too," Lexy agrees.

Dyatlov comes back from the front of the car. He grabs his canteen and takes a big drink.

"Oh, you guys should come meet these guys. They're great! They're heading up to Petrozavodsk for maneuvers. I—" Dyatlov spots Georgi who is soundly sleeping. "Hey! Georgi! Wake up, damn it! What are you, hibernating? Wake up. You're missing all the fun. You're wasting the day."

The group explodes with laughter.

Dyatlov thinks they're laughing at Georgi. "Ha! Yeah, come on you sleepy cow. Wake up!"

A few hours later, the train chugs into the tiny station in the snow-covered village of Vizhai. It's a tiny hamlet of just a few hundred people. The train pulls into the station, and the team jumps off, gathers their gear, and wanders into the main street of the village.

Rusty fishes a note out of his pocket. "Let's see. They say the truck place is just across the street."

"I don't see any trucks. Damn, Rusty, we're wasting what little daylight is left." Dyatlov has been cooped up too long. He hops around.

"What did you tell them?" Zina asks.

Rusty is at a loss. "I said we'd be here, I told them what time the train was arriving."

Alex checks his watch. "Well, we're right on time."

At the end of the tiny street, a large, beat-up truck, surplus from the War, rumbles around the corner, its wheels wrapped in snow chains. The horn honks, and the group runs to it.

39

"Here we go! Hello!" The driver, an old thin man, bundled in thick clothes, stops and opens the back gate. The team crowds in, throwing their packs and skis into the truck. Rusty pays the driver, closes the tailgate, and climbs in.

Nick playfully calls out, "Let the expedition begin!"

"See, there you go. You just have to relax, Dyatlov," Rusty says.

Georgi can't find a seat, so he plops down on the pile of bags. "Not one of his strong suits," Georgi adds.

"No kidding," Nick mumbles.

The students' laughter is drowned out as the truck grinds gears and heads up a tiny road out of the village. The snowy little town is nearly silent as the rumble of the truck fades into the cold evening.

Winter 2009.

Yuri is roughly awakened when one of the city workers kicks the crate he has fallen asleep on.

"Let's go, buddy. This isn't a hotel."

Yuri climbs up. He's used to being rousted and offers no protest. There's no point. He shuffles away, it's now dawn, and more people are out and about. The street crew brings their equipment topside, and a backhoe moves in to fill the hole in the road. Yuri walks through the neighborhood, bundled as tightly as he can manage, trying to keep the heat trapped in his clothes as long as possible. The weather, however, has turned, and wind rips at anything vertical.

Yuri works his way through a massive Soviet-era housing block and goes beyond it through a gulley and into a break of land overgrown with weeds and leafless trees. He crosses an icy meadow and finally arrives at an abandoned neighborhood of large, derelict buildings.

Yuri is cautious and quiet. A gang of bundled up teenagers, obviously on an unauthorized detour on the way to school, runs around throwing bottles and making general mischief. Yuri watches from the snow-filled bushes until the kids take off into the early morning. He slinks through the abandoned neighborhood, ever vigilant lest someone might be watching him. He pauses frequently and lets the early morning settle into silence.

Finally, Yuri finds his home, a huge old building wrapped in dead weeds, junk, and several inches of snow. Yuri carefully moves a couple of wood pallets and a ruined mattress from against a wall of the building to reveal a sizable hole. He re-covers the hole after he wiggles inside. Yuri walks through a short hall, strewn with debris, and rounds the corner into a massive room that perhaps was once a lobby or parlor in an upscale office. Yuri tosses twigs and paper into a tiny makeshift stove. He lights the paper and uses the same match to light a tiny oil lamp.

Yuri wraps himself in a thick sleeping bag. Sitting back in an old chair, he pulls his sleeping bag up under his chin. He moves the lantern close to the wall to illuminate a room papered ceiling to floor with documents, photos, letters, headlines, photocopies, notes, and diagrams. It is the nerve center of his half-century obsession.

The articles and clippings chronicle the events and fallout from the incident fifty years ago. Yuri has hung them in a loose chronology. From the dozens of aged and wrinkled clippings the story emerges: *NINE SKIERS MISSING IN URALS; SEARCH FOR NINE STUDENT SKIERS INTENSIFIES FELLOW STUDENTS AID IN SEARCH; MOSCOW SENDS AID TO SEARCH FOR MISSING HIKERS; FIVE OF THE DYATLOV TEAM FOUND DEAD, REMAINING FOUR PRESUMED DEAD; MYSTERY SURROUNDS THE*

DYATLOV TEAM DEATHS.

Yuri spreads some documents in his lap and opens a book to a place he's marked. He peels open a can of sardines, shakes off some ice crystals, and eats them as he flips through the book. He sifts through a pile of articles and clippings in the pages of the book. The top clipping is titled REPORTS OF ORANGE LIGHTS IN THE SKY PERSIST IN THE URALS. He lingers on a photo of a massive search effort in a huge, snowy meadow.

The Ural Mountains near Mt. Orton. March 13, 1959

It is mid-morning on the face of a snowy, open slope surrounded by tall, snow-covered pine trees. It's bright and sunny but still very cold. A company of Soviet soldiers, volunteers, and police slog through waist-deep snow. In a long line, searchers methodically comb the area, as search dogs struggle in the deep snow. Two Soviet helicopters hover over the area, blowing the snow around as the searchers on the ground prod the snow with long metal poles.

At the far end of the search line, Private Kolar and Private Misha, two young army recruits, stumble as they slog along. They pant and struggle with their large metal searching poles. They are both beat. Kolar is out of breath, as he puffs a continual cloud of vapor in the icy air. He stops. His hat falls off, and he snatches it up and crams it on his head for tenth time.

"This is ridiculous! We aren't going to find shit if we can't even walk," Kolar grumbles.

Private Misha struggles behind Kolar. "Shut up."

Misha tries to step and falls onto his side. "Damn it. I'm freezing. I'm going to freeze to death. Meanwhile, these kids are probably in a cabin a few kilometers away—screwing. I'm telling you, I'm going to freeze!"

"You're not going to freeze," says Kolar. "I'm sweating, you're sweating. I think you'd have to stop sweating before you froze to death. This is absurd. They were reported to be on skis. Shouldn't we be searching on skis, too?"

"Do you even know how to ski?" Misha asks, gasping for breath.

"Not really. But it couldn't be any worse than this." Kolar looks around and can't see the search party. The young soldiers are in a depression in the snow just out of sight of the moving search line.

"I'm going to take a leak," Kolar says.

Misha looks around, nervously. "What? Sergeant Chertoff has got it in for you. Don't piss him off, or you'll be in the stockade."

"Hey, I gotta piss, right?"

The soldiers break off from the end of the line. They slink off and slide into a cover of trees. The snow is thin under the trees and creates a natural shelter. They lean on a thick tree limb, exhausted. Kolar turns around and pees.

Misha takes a pack of cigarettes from inside his coat and lights up. He gripes to Kolar. "What in the hell am I doing here? This is my mother's stupid idea. I never wanted this!"

Kolar zips up. "What else would you do? What, were you going to stock bottles all day and clean up puke at night?"

"Hey, being a bartender wasn't that bad. Plus you can really meet women."

Kolar scratches his head vigorously. "Uhhhh! These damn hats make my head itch! I don't know. Hanging out with bar crowds can get old."

"That's not *all* I was going to do, but it was good for awhile. I'm young. I could do anything. But for the time being I was having fun. But then my mother just kept hammering away at me. 'Do like your brother. Look at how well he's done. Join the army. There's no war on. Look at your brother.' And all of the sudden I'm stuck in the goddamn army. And the infantry no less. I —Oh shit!"

Misha scrambles back. Just a few feet from where they rest are two frozen bodies wearing only long underwear.

"What the hell?" Kolar fumbles and claws at his coat. He finally takes a whistle from inside his coat and blows it with all his might.

The two men struggle from the cover of the tree through the snow and out into the meadow, frantically calling to the search detail. The word is quickly passed down the line, and the troops back track to the spot.

A Russian helicopter turns and hovers over the advancing detail of men. A sergeant pushes through the gawking men to Kolar and Misha, who stand by the tree.

"What have we got here? You," he yells to Kolar. "Report."

"Sir, Private Misha and I discussed what we would do if we were stuck in the snow. We made for these trees. We slid under the branches and found these two. We didn't go near them or touch anything."

The sergeant isn't paying attention to Kolar. He studies the two bodies.

Back in the open meadow, soldiers scramble out

of the way as a huge Soviet helicopter hovers over the show, whipping a swirling cloud of snow and ice. Several men jump from the hovering helicopter and sink into the deep snow. They slog toward the trees. An army major and two plainclothes men push to the front of the searchers who have gathered around the two bodies.

Soldiers look on and speculate.

"Looks like they were trying to make a fire when they died. There's a little pit. And look. He's holding branches."

"Look at their eyes. Is that normal?"

"What the hell is on their skin? They look so old. I thought these were supposed to be kids."

"Maybe it's someone else."

Major Dorskey, who landed in the helicopter, issues a firm order. "Everyone move back. Captain, have your men regroup and comb this area. No one disturb anything."

The KGB men quietly converse, looking at the bodies. They study the scene. One of them, a bald, stern man with a thick hat and a heavy black coat, speaks to the major. "So, major, what do you think?"

The major can't take his eyes off the bodies. They seem pitiful and it disgusts him. One is in his long underwear, his arms tightly folded and his head tucked in. He lies on his side, giving the gathered men a perfect view of his distorted face. The eyes are dried and look like cooked egg whites, and the skin on his face is leathery. His lips have peeled back from his bright white teeth. The dead man has a gold tooth deep in his mouth.

The second man is leaning against a tree, staring up at nothing. His face is delicately dusted with a layer of frost. His eyes are the same as the first man's, and his skin, like that of the first man has an orange tint. Under his wool cap, his hair is white and soft. His hands grip two small tree branches.

"What do I think?" the major says. "I think that you should call someone more important than you or me."

Teams move in to photograph the scene, take measurements, and search for physical evidence.

The rest of the searchers congratulate Misha and Kolar, but the break is brief. The searchers are ordered to sweep to the east and continue. The sad scene, hidden in the snow and pine needles, is left as it was found for most of the day, as the site is examined over and over, again and again.

Finally, as the sun sets, the military and the local police have concluded their investigations, and the order is handed down to move the bodies. Their identities confirmed, the bodies, frozen in position, are clumsily covered with blankets, strapped to gurneys, and taken from the base of the tree. A line of soldiers passes the two corpses out of the trees into the open field. A Soviet helicopter hovers over the snow, waiting as the bodies move along from soldier to soldier.

The engines of the massive helicopter roar, and the rotor blade kicks up snow as the soldiers pass the gurneys along. The pilot sits in the cockpit, watching through his side port as the bodies approach. The prop wash from the spinning rotor easily flings the flimsy blankets off the bodies, revealing the frozen corpses, stiffly posed like broken mannequins.

Fear crawls up the neck of the pilot, who watches the soldiers struggle in the snow as the two contorted bodies head toward the cargo door. The pilot flips on the intercom and talks to the crew in the back.

"Close the door. We have to take off at once."

The copilot, unable to see the bodies, does a double take. "Is there a problem?" he asks.

The crewman at the back door is also puzzled. He calls back into the intercom, "Uhhh...sir, we haven't loaded the cargo yet."

"We're not bringing them on board. Close the door."

The copilot is befuddled. He looks around to see if there's a warning light he has somehow missed. "What's going on, captain?"

The pilot ignores the copilot.

The bodies are ten feet from the helicopter when the crewman starts to close the door.

On the ground, an army major steps up. He grabs the door and holds it. He yells over the engine noise, "Where the hell are you going?"

"I don't know. We just got orders," the crewman yells back.

"But we haven't loaded yet. Whose goddamn orders?"

"I don't know. The captain says we have to go. Now."

The major starts to call into his radio and tries to hold the huge helicopter. "Wait! Hang on! Just wait!"

But the chopper's powerful motor revs up. The crewman apologetically shrugs and closes the door. The engine roars, and the snow blasts the entire detail. The soldiers stand around, holding the twisted bodies on the two gurneys.

"Sir, what do we do with these...bodies?"

"We walk them down to the truck. About face. Let's go."

Inside the helicopter the crewman watches the scene below him fade into white. He calls into his intercom, "Sir, that Major down there wasn't too pleased. What happened? What is the urgent order?"

"Fuel lines started to freeze that close to the ground. We had to go."

The copilot looks at the captain and can see he's bathed in sweat. He says nothing but turns away and scoffs to himself. He knows the pilot is superstitious, but had no idea that it went to this level.

The soldier at the cargo door is still confused. "Fuel lines, captain? I've never heard of that. I don't understand."

The captain snaps back over the intercom. "No one cares what you do or don't understand. Got it?"

"Yes, sir."

The helicopter leaves the mountain area and returns to the base, reporting unspecific mechanical problems.

April 23, 1959.

Young Yuri sits in his dorm room studying. His roommate, Titov, sits studying as well. Titov is young and tall, with a square face, and tiny glasses over his bright blue eyes. He fidgets and squirms as he studies.

"Ugh. Algebra. I loathe Algebra."

Yuri looks up from his books. "Are you joking? You're a math major."

"I know, but my focus is going to be on geometry. And it's not that I can't do it. I just don't like doing it. Geometry has practical applications. It's elegant."

Yuri turns back to his books. "I don't know how you could do either. Math bores me to tears."

"Sometimes I don't know how I can do it either. C'mon, Yuri. Let's go find some girls and go dancing."

Yuri doesn't even look up. "No, I think I've cleared enough bars for a while."

"What do you mean?"

Yuri throws Titov a glance. "You know what I mean."

Titov is dismissive. "Forget them. Stupid girls. So easily spooked. It's insane."

"It wasn't just the girls. It was everyone in the place. I'm a curse, Tee. I'm bad luck. Hell, ask anybody, everybody."

"Aw, to hell with them. Superstitious idiots. What is this, the dark ages? You be thankful you weren't with them, or you'd be…well…missing, number ten." Titov dances around the obvious.

Somehow Yuri is still optimistic about his lost friends. "They could be OK," Yuri mutters. "Maybe someone got hurt and they had to hole up in a cabin or something?"

Titov has tried to stay optimistic, but it's just been too long. "Seriously? Two—almost three—months? Georgi and Alex would never have missed their exams. Dyatlov wouldn't have missed his thesis demonstration if he had to drag his smashed body across a desert."

"That's a lovely image." Yuri takes out a flask from his closet. He takes a big swig. He hands it to Titov, who takes a drink as well.

"Whatever happened, it's seriously shitty. What do you think happened, Yuri?"

Yuri thinks but has no answer. "I don't know… I…I…I don't know. A storm? Got lost?"

Titov is skeptical. "Dyatlov and Lexy? Those guys were more comfortable outdoors than in. And Georgi too. And Nick get lost? Hell, he made maps."

52

Yuri nods in agreement. "You're right. Hell, I don't know."

Titov takes another swig. "So damn weird. And I hate to state the obvious, but they've got to be…you know… dead. By now. There's just no way."

"Yeah, I know." Yuri looks out the window.

"Sasha Labedka's mom asked my mom to ask you if you saw any spirits or had any premonitions—before you guys left."

"Mmmm…No, not really." Yuri doesn't sound too confident.

"Not really?"

"Well, when I was coming back down—after I got sick—I skied through that Mansi camp—where we'd been earlier."

The same place where Dyatlov smacked that guy? Titov asks.

"Yes, just one day later. In fact, I followed our own tracks back," Yuri explains.

"And?"

"Well, when I got there, they were gone. The whole tribe. Gone. All that was left was a few empty sod huts. I also found the stuff we'd given them. They'd given us some reindeer meat, so we wanted to give them something, too. Anyway, the stuff we'd given them— some bread, a couple pieces of fruit, a comb. I found it all, half burned in their fire pit."

"Really?" Titov is intrigued.

"Really. And then when I got down to Vizhai, I felt like total garbage, sick as a dog. I got on the train, and as I was heading back, I sort of knew. I mean I felt this sickening certainty I've never felt before."

Titov studies Yuri closely. He smiles wryly. "Are you pulling my leg?"

"No, I'm not. I felt horrible because…you know…I was sick, but even beyond that, I sort of got the idea that someone was…going to—"

A deep voice speaks up from the doorway. "Die?"

Titov and Yuri jump. They thought they were alone. Detective Cosmo Kroll steps into the room. He has been listening in the hall for some time.

Titov is pissed and stands. "What the hell, mister. You shouldn't sneak up on people like that."

"It's not 'mister;' it's 'detective,'" the detective corrects. The inspector, average height with black hair and a rough complexion, wears a thick a moustache and neat goatee. His dark eyes study everything. His air of calm is unsettling to Yuri and Titov. He's very mild and soft spoken. Cosmo motions Titov to sit down. He spots the flask on the counter.

"Isn't this a dry dorm?" Titov picks it up and tucks it into his pocket.

"It's medicinal," Titov says with an air of contempt.

Cosmo smirks. "I'll bet. Tell you what, why don't you leave me alone with your roommate here."

Titov isn't intimidated by the detective. "Ummmm…I don't really want to, actually."

Yuri takes the defiant cue. "I really don't want him to leave. I don't have anything to say to you that I wouldn't say to Tee."

Cosmo considers them both. "But what if I have something to say to you, something very private?"

No one answers. The silence is awkward.

Cosmo breaks the tension. "Well, why don't you finish your story first? So you met a tribe of the Mansi people on your way up to this…What was it, exactly?"

Yuri breathes a bored sigh. "I've told everyone this—the police, the papers, the KGB, everyone. I spent about two weeks straight going from one interrogation to the next. It was a ski expedition."

"In the dead of winter?"

"Yeah, ski clubs are more effective in winter, what with snow and all that."

Comso smiles at the wisecrack. "So the goal was to just see how tough you are?"

"No, not really, not tough. You know, just see what we could do, push ourselves. Zina, she's going to be an Olympian, maybe—or was."

Cosmo nods. "It's a good Russian trait. It's that attitude that drove out the Nazis. But why up there, to that area?"

"I don't know. Dyatlov picked the route."

"No debate?"

"It wasn't a matter of debate. It was his…his show, his trip. He's club president. If you didn't like what he planned, you didn't go. Pretty straight forward. And if all of us had gotten sick, he'd have gone by himself."

Titov chimes in, "It's true. Dyatlov is a force of nature."

Cosmo takes out a notebook and scribbles. Without looking up, he asks, "You think they're dead?"

Titov shrugs and feels sheepish. "C'mon," he says, "It's been months. Rusty, Nick, and Alex were serious students. They wouldn't have missed their exams, their jobs. No way. None of them would. They would write or wire their parents if they could."

"What if they left the country, slipped out, kept going. They had provisions. What if they set off into Finland?"

Titov is shocked and laughs out loud. "What,

you think they defected?"

"People defect, it happens," Cosmo says.

"No way, not them. I mean they weren't rank-and-file Soviets, but they were rooted here," Titov says. "And Dyatlov was the best little soviet there ever was. I think he wanted to be on your team someday."

Cosmo continues to take notes. "I'm not on any team. I'm just asking questions. But that bothers you about *Comrade* Dyatlov?"

"It doesn't bother me. It's just an observation," Titov answers.

"And you said that this feeling of dread—" Cosmo turns to Yuri. "You felt someone was going to die. Is that right?"

"It sounds…strange, but yes." Yuri is a little embarrassed. "I did feel that, but I was sick with the flu."

"Well, sadly, you were right. I'm sorry to report that they have found five of them dead."

Yuri covers his face with his hands as Titov reels in shock.

Yuri mumbles to the inspector, "Oh no, I knew it."

"Who is it?" Titov asks.

The detective studies the two men. "We need to tell their families first."

Yuri gets up and paces. He grabs a glass of water, and he shakes uncontrollably.

"This isn't…this isn't…Oh my God…Do you know about…What about…Lyudy? I mean, Lyudmila?"

"Your girlfriend?"

"My friend. Since we were kids," Yuri corrects the detective.

"No, Lyudmila Dubinina wasn't among them, but, suffice it to say, it's just a matter of time. I'm sorry to be the bearer of bad news. I'll call on you again if I have any more information, and for the time being, I ask that you not share any of this information with anyone. This is an ongoing criminal investigation. Good evening, gentlemen."

Detective Cosmo nods and leaves, his footfalls disappearing down the corridor. Yuri stands and stares out the window. He turns away, hiding the tears that freely run down his face.

Three weeks later, on the other side of Moscow, a group of military and police investigators gathers in the morgue of a large military hospital. The room is tiled in white, with rows of buzzing fluorescent lights and banks of large metal drawers. The stench of bleach and formaldehyde is overpowering, and yet the sweet smell of rot is still evident.

A doctor leads the assembled group down a stark hallway. The men pass through several sets of double doors and end up in a large autopsy theatre.

Four bodies, covered with sheets, are lined up on rolling metal gurneys. Medical personnel disperse as the men enter the room. Only Dr. Simon Vasili remains.

"Good morning," he says.

"Hello," someone mumbles.

Vasili sees the epaulets of a colonel. "Good morning Colonel."

The colonel stuffs his hands into his pockets and grumbles, "Pretty goddamned melodramatic doing this in the morgue, don't you think?"

A general steps out of the shadows. The general is a huge man and carries himself with the calm power that befits his position. "I thought we should all see for ourselves, colonel. If that's all right with you."

The colonel is caught off guard. "Uh…Of course, General. I just—" The general waves him away.

"Just get on with it," the general says.

Dr. Vasili snaps to. A consummate professional, he speaks with the flat delivery of a man steeped in the scientific method:

"Yes, sir, of course. As everyone knows, nine skiers from a polytechnic college went missing in the Urals at the beginning of February of this year. When the first five bodies were discovered, the cause of death was suspicious enough to warrant a criminal investigation to determine what killed these individuals.

"Ten days ago the remaining bodies of the lost skiers were found. Like the previous five bodies, these bodies also gave off high levels of radioactivity. The clothes, gear, and tents of both groups also showed the same levels of contamination."

A colonel interrupts. "Radioactive? Atomic poisoning? Professor Koliev, can this occur naturally?

Another scientist steps forward. Professor Koliev thinks. "There is natural radioactivity all over the planet, coming up from the earth, but these levels are too high to be of natural origin. And although the levels are elevated, it should be noted that they were not high enough, for such brief exposure, to pose any health risk."

"Why were these students there in the first place?" asks another official.

"Sir," replies an investigator with a clipboard, "it was a planned outing, a ski club, apparently. They wanted to test their skills against nature or something like that. Three of the students also had personal cameras. Two of them were recovered. The film was processed, and nothing out of the ordinary was found in the images. Just as you'd expect, a bunch of athletic kids having fun and taking pictures of their outing.

"All of the dead were members of other outdoor activity clubs as well. And all of them had taken many, many trips before. Two had almost been Olympians in various skiing events. The students had planned to head to Mt. Orton and then to call or wire their families on or about February 11 when they made a circle back to Vizhai. When they didn't immediately wire their families, it was of little concern because they were all such experienced outdoorsmen—and women."

Another officer, a captain, joins in the briefing, reading from a file:

"Some of their friends thought that perhaps they'd gone a more difficult route, but after two weeks, local police got calls from parents, and a search party was assembled. After a lengthy search, the first five bodies were found."

The captain motions toward a topographical map on an easel.

"The first two were found about 600 meters from what was their original camp, on the edge of a forest. They were Georgi Krivonischenko and Yuri Doroshenko. The two dead men were dressed only in their underwear with none of their winter clothing. One was barefoot, and the other had on a single boot. The two died of exposure. There was also evidence at the location that suggested they'd been partially blinded: They had made a tiny fire, that burned briefly, because they used wet wood, and yet failed to notice dried kindling within arm's reach. Broken limbs on a tree suggested that one of the two had climbed a tree, perhaps looking for the camp or others. Because of the time it took to discover the bodies, it's hard to pin point exactly when death occurred, but a reasonable guess is that they died on the night of February 2, between 9:00 p.m. and 6:00 a.m."

The general drops into a wooden seat against a wall. It creaks under his massive weight. "What were they doing in their underwear, outside a tent, in the middle of the night?"

"Unknown, General. Two days later, three more bodies were found, also partially clothed, between the woods and their camp. Two were next to each other, and the woman was roughly 100 meters from the two men. These were the bodies of Igor Dyatlov, Zinaida Kolmogorova, and Rustem Slobodin. It appeared that they had been sharing what little clothing they had. The feet of one victim were wrapped in the jacket liner of another."

The captain signals an orderly near the door to turn off the lights. The captain flips on a slide projector. Slides from the scene light up a small screen and illustrate what he's talking about. The first image shows a photo of a body in the snow, with feet sticking out and coat liner wrapped around a foot.

"There was also evidence that suggested that they had tried to take clothes from those already dead and that some of the more able members may have tried to help the more seriously injured."

The major speaks up. "From the positions of these bodies and the tracks, we've determined that the group was most likely heading back up the slope, toward the original camp, when they died. A flashlight was found tied to a tent pole back at the base camp."

"What was that for?" asks another.

"Perhaps one of them was trying to signal the rest," suggests someone else. "It was a blizzard, right?

Trying to show them how to get back to camp."

The captain flips through a few pages on his clipboard. "Meteorological data suggests that it was near-blizzard conditions on that night and on the next two nights."

"But why in the hell did they leave the camp in the first place?" The colonel is baffled.

The major continues. "Unknown. All died of hypothermia in what would have been well below freezing conditions. Igor Dyatlov did have a small skull contusion, although forensics concluded that it was superficial."

The room is abuzz. Nothing is making any sense to anyone.

The general rubs his eyes, hoping to soothe his pounding headache. "Why in the hell would such experienced hikers camp on an unprotected slope when there was forest so close by?"

"Unknown, sir," Replies the major. "A driving storm may have forced the team to camp where they had stopped, or perhaps they wanted to practice camping in more challenging conditions. As stated, at the discovery of the first set of bodies, a criminal inquest was started. Next slide please. Of course there is no way to be 100 percent sure, but the tent appeared to have been cut open from the inside, suggesting that something had awakened the team and was blocking the normal entrance."

"What would make them do that?" someone asks. "A wild animal? A pack of wolves? Maybe a bear coming through the flap? Are there bears in that area?"

The captain answers the question. "No evidence of any tracks other than those of the victims. No coyote, deer, wolf, bear, or humans. Nothing."

"Why were they all in one tent to begin with?"

"Unknown. At the camp, their food, skis, and equipment were found abandoned. No bodies were found at the camp."

The captain motions toward the bodies on the gurneys. "These are the bodies found last week, and the entire team is now accounted for. Incidentally, one more student left the trip early because he had come down with the flu. He is Yuri Yudin, and he was questioned thoroughly and dismissed."

"Lucky bastard. I read about him," someone mumbles.

The general prods the doctor. "Doctor, would you continue?"

Vasili crosses to the X-ray viewer. He turns on the lights, and the X-rays blink to life. "This is the film of Nicholas Thibeaux-Brignollel a pre-med student. The skull, as you can see here, was crushed. The sixth and seventh vertebrae are severely damaged, and several other vertebrae have fractures. The victim has numerous broken ribs and other bone fractures, several of which are compound. This of course is all in line with the massive injuries to the internal organs: lungs, liver. There is moderate to heavy damage to almost every major organ."

The colonel studies the films. He mutters, "Good God, it's as if he were run over by a tank."

"How about those Mansi people" another officer asks. "What do we know about them? Perhaps the kids desecrated some sacred land and the Mansi attacked them?"

The major speaks up. "We investigated the Mansi thoroughly when the first bodies were discovered. They had no grudge against those kids, and they avoided this area mountain like the plague. They wouldn't go near it. The one surviving student, Yudin, said they had met the Mansi early in the trip. Besides a scuffle between an old man and Igor Dyatlov, they just went on their way."

The general clears his throat. "Doctor, what… what do you…what caused these wounds?"

"That is the troubling part, general," Vasili replies. "There are no obvious indications of any outside force. No sign of external trauma at all. No soft tissue damage. No person could inflict this type of damage without leaving some sort of mark on the outside of the body."

"Then how do you explain it, doctor?" The general is getting a bit annoyed.

The doctor is embarrassed. "I…I can't. I—and not just myself—I and several colleagues were forced to rule the instrument of death as an 'unknown compelling force.'"

The colonel addresses the captain. "Captain, what about where the bodies were found?"

"Brignollel was found with these three: Lolevatov and Zolotarev and the second girl, Dubinina. As you can see from the films, these bodies all show massive internal injuries. They were found further into the forest in a streambed at the bottom of a ravine, buried in deep snow. It seemed as if they had perhaps been lined up, almost side by side, although a state hydrologist thinks the snow melt might have caused them to line up so neatly."

The doctor puts up films of Lyudmila. Her ribs are completely crushed.

The general gets up, crosses to the wall of X-rays, and studies the images. "I don't mind saying that this is goddamn troubling. I'd really like someone to tell me what in the hell is going on here."

The doctor moves over to the bodies. "That's not the most troubling part." Doctor Vasili pulls back the sheet covering Lyudmila. Her face is twisted into a ghastly shape. Her mouth is peeled wide open, and her jaw is pushed back against her throat. The doctor flips on a bright light and pokes inside the gaping mouth. "I realize that this is graphic, but it is important to see. Notice here: The tongue and all the corresponding muscles are gone."

The major is baffled. "Gone? You mean removed?"

The doctor studies the corpse. "Yes, obviously But then how…It's…It's as if they were never there to begin with, almost as if they were surgically removed."

"Surgery? What could do that?" The confused men struggle with ideas.

"Unknown, general."

"What about a coyote? A wolf? A bear? Maybe crows sat and picked it all apart. They're scavengers."

"We don't think so. As was noted before, there were no animal tracks, and if it had been an animal, there would be teeth marks, torn skin, and signs of chewing. None of that is present."

The General is truly shaken. "Goddamn it! I've seen enough. Cover the poor girl up."

The general gives a nod, and the major picks up a phone and hands it to the general.

The general speaks to the room. "Gentlemen, that will be all."

Everyone quickly disperses.

The general holds the phone in his huge hands, cupping the mouthpiece. He looks sternly at the colonel.

"Colonel, tell me, why wasn't the KGB here today?"

"They sent a message. They were briefed earlier."

"Of course," the general grumbles. The general is a soldier and doesn't mix well with the KGB.

"And they said they'd be looking into it," the colonel adds.

"And who, may I ask, said that?" The general stares at the white sheet over the girl's mangled body.

"He said he was Comrade Leonoav. I don't know him."

"Fucking KGB," the general rumbles. "A damn pit of information. Everything goes in, and nothing comes out. This seems like a weapon. I think someone tested some sort of weapon on these kids. That's what I think. Or maybe they wandered into a test—wrong place at the wrong time."

The colonel considers it. "Perhaps the Americans, the British?"

"Someone. Who knows? Maybe us." The general talks into the phone. "Connect me to the Kremlin."

Days later, in a crowded, smoky pub, friends and family of the dead have gathered after the final funeral for an impromptu wake. The tiny bar, a local haunt for students of the college, is packed but somber. It's uncharacteristically warm, and two tiny desk fans at the window provide little relief. People, slick with perspiration, drink and talk, but their black clothing is a constant reminder of why they are there. On a mantel behind the bar, sits a mishmash photo lineup of the dead students with flowers piled around the pictures.

Two students, Gregory and Hilda, study the pictures.

"Ugh," Hilda murmurs to Gregory. "I think I'm going to go to just one more funeral—mine."

"I know. I hate it. I mean, I knew they were dead. What else? Missing for all that time. They had to be, but still…sitting up there in the snow like that for months…" Gregory shudders at the thought.

"Hey, they weren't feeling any pain. We're the ones left to suffer."

Gregory scans the photos. "Well, they're all

accounted for now. Nick was my roommate freshman year. I didn't know him particularly well. There were six of us that term. But he was a good guy. That was obvious. And Yuri Doroshenko, too."

A group of students sits at a table sipping beers and talking reverently. Marcus, a short, thin student, returns to a table with more beer. Sasha, a plain girl with red hair, fans herself with a napkin. Next to her is Tina. Tina is thin with long black hair, and her eyes, like Sasha's, are puffy and red from crying. Their friend Peter takes a beer from Marcus.

Tina grabs a beer and immediately guzzles half of it.

"Hey, take it easy. You've got a test tomorrow," Marcus reminds her.

Tina stares off into the distance. "Leave me alone. I'm not going to any stupid exam."

Marcus sips his beer and tries to make eye contact with Tina. "Look, she would have wanted you to go on, live your life."

Sasha nods in agreement. She absent-mindedly peels the label off an empty bottle at the table. "It's true," she adds.

Tina appears not to be listening, but she is. And her friends' words of solace only annoy her. "Everyone always says that shit. They'd want you to live your life, soldier on, enjoy what you have. What else would they want? It's stupid to say shit like that." She takes another huge swig of beer. "What do the dead want for us? The real answer is they don't want. They don't want anything. They have no opinion. They're dead. All their wants, all their needs are erased. Just someone else's memory of what they wanted."

"Tina, what are you talking about?" Sasha is

confused.

Peter waves it away. "She's drunk. But I for one want to engage in this theological discussion. So you are suggesting that even if someone wanted something, once they're gone, it's irrelevant? What about a great architect? What about a great musician—Prokofiev, Beethoven? What about values, then? How you raise a child, how you—"

Marcus interrupts. "Damn, Peter. Does everything have to be a stupid debate with you?"

Sasha agrees. "I think you're being very disrespectful of the departed. And I don't think this is the place for such a debate."

Now Peter is annoyed with the others. "You're both drunk. I was just trying to maybe change the subject or something."

Tina drops her head, sobbing. "They cut out her tongue. All of it. Torn out of her mouth."

Marcus rubs Tina's back. "Don't. Come on now, Tina. Don't. Don't do it. It's not... You know how you get. You know how obsessed you can get. She was your friend. It's not healthy to dwell on those details."

Sasha puts her arm around Tina's shoulders. "He's right, Tina. Don't dwell on her death. Think about her when she was alive and happy. She'd want you to remember her that way."

Tina blubbers between sobs, "You're doing it again with the 'she would want' nonsense."

"That's all rumors anyway," Marcus adds. "People are so easily spooked. It's ridiculous. Do you know Hova? Hova's grandmother thinks they were killed by the Devil. And some of their own mothers must have thought so too. Rusty, Zina, Alex? Their own mothers wouldn't walk alongside the caskets."

Peter is still thinking about the missing tongue. "There are coyotes in those hills. It's very...well...unpleasant to think about, but that's probably what took... I mean, you know...ate her tongue. My uncle did oil exploration up there," Peter continues. "He said that those Mansi people won't go near that area. A bunch of their people mysteriously died up there too."

Another student leans over. He's been listening. He's looks like a wrestler. "All this mysterious bullshit? It's an avalanche. Simple. An avalanche buried the tent. They carved themselves out. Kolevatov and what's-his-name got hit by the full impact of the snow, causing the severe internal injuries."

"What about the tongue?" Tina asks.

"Were you there? Have you seen this removed tongue? We only know what they tell the papers—and the stupid rumors."

Marcus dismisses the avalanche theory. "Well, you don't know your geography, because that mountain isn't a mountain it's more of a big flat area *in* the mountains, and you've got to have some serious angles for an avalanche. There aren't any mountains like that in that area. It's simple physics."

Unbeknownst to the drinkers, Yuri Yudin sits alone behind the group in a small booth, listening. Yuri drinks the last of his beer and puts down a coin.

Marcus notices as Yuri leaves. He slides down in his seat. "Awwwwwh, shit."

"What? What's wrong?" Sasha asks.

"That guy. That guy who just left? It was Yudin. Yuri Yudin."

"Seriously? Yudin?" Tina looks around.

"He heard everything we said. I had no idea he was—"

70

"That's horrible. Poor guy," Sasha says.

"To hell with him," Peter says. "He's heard it all by now anyway. He should be thankful to be alive. And he says he saw them alive, but did anyone else? Who knows what 'condition' they were in when he left?"

Tina empties her beer. "Peter, you're such an ass."

The following evening is still unpleasantly warm, even as the dusty, orange sun sets. Yuri, now determined to find answers, decides to ditch his classes for the next few days. He waits until Titov is at the library and then heads to the train station. With his backpacking gear over his shoulder, he buys a ticket and walks to the platform. Yuri drops onto a bench and tries to calm down. He closes his eyes and breathes deeply. He can't remember the last time he slept well. All the looks, the stares, the accusations, and the racking guilt that he left Lyudmila up there to die plagues him. He breathes deeply and tries to shake himself loose from his thoughts even for just a moment.

Almost immediately, an old man, sits down next to him. Yuri rolls his eyes. Sitting too close to him is a white-haired man, spotted with perspiration and stinking of body odor. He wears a moth-eaten shirt, ratty pants and worn leather sandals. The old man takes a swig off a bottle.

Uncomfortable, Yuri takes out a textbook and pretends to read. The old man, apparently wanting to chat, offers Yuri a sip. Yuri tries to ignore him, but he wags the bottle in Yuri's face. Yuri tries to refuse politely, but the old man won't give up. Finally, Yuri gives in and takes a small, symbolic sip. The old man laughs.

"Thanks, thanks a lot," Yuri says.

The old man smiles broadly and pats Yuri's arm. "No problem. Now we're friends! You'd do the same for me."

"Sure, I would," Yuri replies.

The old man yawns and scratches. "So where are you headed?" he asks as he passes the bottle back to Yuri.

"Vizhai. I'm going to do a little hiking in—"

Without warning, the old man snatches his bottle from Yuri's mouth just as he's about to sip. The man stands up and walks away, never looking back. Yuri is stunned. He sits back, not sure what just happened. He stands and looks for the old man, but his train pulls into the station. Yuri boards the train, still pondering. The train leaves the station as the sun disappears behind the horizon.

Early the next morning, Yuri is sleeping awkwardly across three seats on the train. The car is empty, except for a young woman and a boy, who sleep next to one another.

The PA system crackles to life. "Next stop, Vizhai. Calling next at Asbest and Beryozovsky. Next stop, Vizhai." Yuri sits up, twists his back, and shakes off the lousy night's sleep.

It's almost summer in the Ural Mountains, but a storm has moved in. Yuri grumbles at the steady rain. He finds his rain poncho, puts on his backpack, and pulls the poncho over himself and the pack. He steps off the train.

In the early morning, the tiny village is quiet. Yuri walks from the small train station into the village. The village looks different than it did in winter. Trees, weeds, and wildflowers are everywhere.

Vizhai consists of a few humble businesses, a

few houses, a store, and a small café. One paved road, cracked and full of puddles, is the main street. Yuri yawns and heads into the small restaurant.

The ancient café is empty. It's a tiny place with peeling wood paneling and a few mismatched tables and chairs. Still the smell of cooking food wafts through the door as Yuri enters. A bell rings on the top of the old door, and a middle-aged woman appears from the kitchen.

"Hello and good morning," Yuri offers.

The woman, still wearing her apron, wipes her hands with a towel. "What can I do for you?" she asks quietly.

"Yes, I was wondering if I could get a meat pie or some soup? Do you have soup this early?"

She walks over to him, but when she gets close enough to see Yuri, her demeanor changes. The woman seems suddenly nervous and looks about, trying to not meet Yuri's eye.

"I'm sorry. We're closed" she says abruptly.

"Oh…uh…What time do you open?"

"I'm…No, we're not opening today. I'm sorry. Family emergency. I have to take care of…my daughter. I'm sorry."

Yuri can feel the tension. "Oh, of course. All right. I'm sorry to hear that. Um…Do you have a loaf of bread or something that I can buy and take with—"

"No, I'm sorry. The kitchen is all locked up. You'll have to go. I'm sorry."

Yuri is baffled. "Er…OK…I…OK, I'm sorry. Good morning, then."

As Yuri starts to leave, three burly men come in laughing and joking. "Don't bother. They're closed," he says.

"What? They never close. Ushy! We demand sausages. And water for our horses and a big trout for my fishy friend, Herman!"

Herman playfully protests. "You're the fish, not me! Smell his breath!"

They all laugh and push past Yuri. Yuri walks away from the café and watches. Inside, the men sit down at a table.

He adjusts his backpack and walks down the street to the small trucking company he and his friends had hired in the winter. The owner is just rolling up the steel gate to the office. He talks to Yuri without looking at him.

"Can I help you, son?"

"Yes sir, good morning. I was wondering if I could get a ride up to the base of the mountain, I don't know if you remember me. You drove me and my friends up the mountain a few months ago—"

The truck driver still won't look at Yuri. "Can't say that I do. I drive a lot of people around."

"I'm…I'm sure you do. I've got money. So if…I mean…What time does the next bus or truck leave?"

The truck driver pulls oilcans out of a cabinet. "It doesn't."

"I'm sorry?" Yuri doesn't understand.

The truck driver is annoyed with Yuri and doesn't hide it. "There is no transportation going up the mountain. That area is all closed off."

"Closed off? Closed off by whom?" Yuri asks.

"Well, who do you think has the authority to close off a whole mountain? "Hmm?" Yuri tries to protest. "I just—"

"I know who you are, Yuri Yudin. But there's nothing up there for you. You need to leave now. You need to be on that next train, son. For your own good."

Yuri is perturbed and can feel his face reddening. "What do you know about my own good?"

"I've got work to do."

"Look, can I just ask you—"

The truck driver turns away from Yuri, heads into his tiny office, and shuts the door behind him. Yuri stands alone in street. He is now suspicious and disgusted. "So they know all about me," he thinks. "Well, good for them. Damn superstitious peasants."

Yuri is angry but more determined than ever. He takes a drink from his canteen, adjusts his poncho, cinches up the straps on his backpack, and starts to walk toward the road leading into the mountains. As he rounds the last buildings that define the village, a voice calls out to him.

"Not really the best day to go hiking. It's as if we are in a cloud—with all this water."

Yuri stops and turns around. "Excuse me?"

A man stands on the porch of a small building. He's dressed in a smart suit. He's short with slicked-back blonde hair, sharp features, and thick glasses. The man steps out from under the protection of the porch and puts on a wide-brimmed black hat.

"I said it's not really a good time for mountain activities, considering—"

"Considering what?" Yuri calls back. It's obvious to him that the man is a KGB operative.

"Considering the last time you went on an outing 90 percent of the party wound up dead." The man walks into the road. He stands in front of Yuri.

Yuri is defiant. "What do you know about that?" Rain soaks Yuri's face and hair.

Drops fall from the brim of the man's hat. He

steps even closer, but Yuri doesn't back up. Two more agents get out of a black sedan parked behind the small building. The smartly dressed man thinks for a long, awkward moment, sizing Yuri up. Finally, he speaks very softly. He's so close that Yuri can smell his sour breath. "You ask a lot of questions for someone who should be answering them."

Yuri finally backs up.

"Go ahead. Ask. Because then I've got about a thousand goddamn questions myself. And I've told my story so many times. You know what I know. Tell me, was Igor Dyatlov working for you? Did he take us up there on your orders?"

The agent ignores Yuri's question. "Do you consider yourself a good student, Yuri Yudin?" he asks.

Yuri laughs. "Haven't you checked my records yet? To make sure I'm the model Soviet?"

The agent puts his hands in his coat pockets and sighs deeply. "There you go with the questions again. Tell you what, you ask me one more question, and I promise you that you will not be able to stand up for at least thirty minutes. Now, do you, Yuri Yudin, consider yourself a good student?" His tone has turned menacing.

Yuri swallows hard. "Yes. Yes, I do."

"Do you pay your taxes, your tuitions?" the agent continues.

"Of course."

"Take care of your family? Your brother? Your mother?"

Yuri agrees to all of it.

"Then you work for us, too. Because that's what good citizens do. That's how you work for the government, and the government works for you. We're all the same. We all work for each other. That is what makes this country of ours so great. I would have thought you'd have learned all this in basic Soviet history." He studies Yuri. "Now, when you stop being a good citizen, then you work against everyone else. It's not fair to all the good citizens when someone else isn't being good—like poking around a crime scene, for instance."

Yuri is scared but determined not to show it. "I can't believe this. If you know anything, you know I wasn't anywhere near there when they disappeared."

"I wasn't there. No one was. No one lived to say who was where. In fact, all we have is what you've said. You were the last person to see them alive, and now you're here again."

"Look, I just want to know what happened. They were my friends. I have a right to know what killed them."

The agent smiles a big, cold smile. "See, we're so similar, you and I. Because that is exactly what I want to know, too."

Yuri tries to add something, but the agent cuts him off.

"Look, son, I feel for you. I do. I really do. You seem like a good enough kid. And I know that you want to ask me lots of questions, but then you would miss your train. Because you'd be lying up here, unable to get up."

The moment is awkward. The agent doesn't move. He simply rocks on his heels, never taking his gaze off Yuri. Yuri shifts and squirms. Finally, the agent motions toward the train station.

"I think you can help yourself to tea, coffee, and biscuits inside the train station."

Yuri gets the message—loud and clear. He studies the agents as they watch him.

Without saying a word, Yuri walks back down through the tiny hamlet and into the train station. The KGB men follow at a distance. Yuri begrudgingly enters the station and sits on a bench. He looks up toward where he would have gone, toward the mountain now hidden in a bank of thick rain clouds.

2009.

It's late morning but still dark and cold outside.
Yuri is waking up in his derelict house. He folds back
layers and layers of blankets and a sleeping bag. He
stands up and stretches. He sips the last cold tea from a
tiny teapot on the makeshift stove, still glowing faintly.
A bucket of water is at the edge of the room. Yuri lifts
out the top frozen layer and then splashes his face with
water from the bucket. He fishes a toothbrush from a
cup and quickly brushes his teeth.

Yuri roots around in his coat pocket and pulls
out his watch. He's late. Suddenly in a hurry, Yuri
dresses as he scrambles around. He moves some floor-
boards and reaches deep into a hole. He pulls out a can
and dumps a small amount of money onto the bed.
From another secret spot he pulls out more cash. He
smoothes the bills, then folds the wad, and stuffs it into
his pocket. He finishes dressing and heads out through
the concealed hole in the wall. Instinctively, Yuri pauses
and waits to see if anyone is watching or passing by.

Satisfied that he is alone, he moves out into the morning and quickly conceals his secret entrance.

Outside the huge stone building, the snow swirls around. Yuri folds up his collar, pulls down his hats, and heads off into the gray winter morning.

An hour later, Yuri stomps the snow from his boots on the porch of a small working-class bar. Inside the sad little place, a few men drink while two others play pool. Other men watch a soccer match on a TV whose colors are wildly out of tune, but the men don't seem to notice or care. Sitting alone at a small table, dressed in a bright-yellow running suit, is Anders, a sickly, bald middle-aged man with horrible teeth

Yuri steps in the door and shakes off the cold. Immediately, the bartender spots him and lays into him.

"Hey, you! Nope. Sorry. You aren't welcome. Keep moving."

Yuri flashes some money, and the bartender calms down.

"Well, all right, but no bathing in the rest room. I've cleaned up after too many of you swine."

Yuri nods faintly and walks toward Anders. "Hello, Anders?"

"Shit, grampy. Where the hell you been?"

"Oh...I...uh...sorry." Yuri is apologetic.

"Well, sit down, man. Sit down."

"Oh, sorry. Sure." Yuri pulls out a chair and sits down.

"OK, good. That's better. Let's relax for a second. OK?" Anders is fidgety and nervous.

"Just calm down a bit." Yuri isn't the least bit nervous and glances around to see if the Anders is still talking to him.

Anders continues with his nervous babble.

"Whewwww. You're filthy, you know that? You should take more pride in your appearance."

Yuri looks at himself. "Uh…OK? I guess," Yuri mumbles.

"You want something to drink?"

Yuri looks around, trying to figure out if the bar has food. "Uh…soup?" Yuri asks.

"I think they got booze and maybe water or a Coca-Cola or something like that," Anders says.

"Oh…uh…lemon soda?"

Anders catches the attention of a tired waitress reading the paper at the bar. She drags herself to their table.

"Great. Here she comes. Hi...er…Excuse me, but can I get another pint? And he'll have a lemon soda."

"OK, that'll be 4 and 20," she sighs, holding out her hand.

"Ok…uh…Go ahead." Anders turns to Yuri.

They sit in silence for a moment. Yuri finally notices. "Oh, I pay for this too? Then I guess this is for you." He hands the waitress the coins. She shuffles off as Anders looks around.

"OK, pops, give me the cash." Anders holds out his shaking hands.

Yuri winces. He leans in and whispers to Anders, "Maybe I should hand it under the table."

Anders catches Yuri's meaning and is suddenly paranoid. He hunches over and whispers to Yuri, "Oh, yeah, right. Under the table."

Yuri casually passes the wad under the table, but Anders is too nervous and has to peek under the table twice before finding Yuri's hand. Anders takes the money, tries to stuff it in the pocket of his running suit, and spills half the bills onto the floor. He hastily gathers them up.

Yuri sighs and almost laughs as the waitress comes with their drinks. Anders is bumbling and obvious, but the waitress couldn't care less. She sets down the drinks.

"Beer and lemon soda."

"Oh…er…Thank you." Anders tries to act casual.

"Yes, thank you," Yuri adds.

Anders watches until the waitress is gone and then whispers to Yuri, "I have to be careful. I've been to jail. It's no picnic. This is certain. OK, so here's the plan: You meet her tonight at midnight. She takes a smoke break out one of the fire exits in the back alley. She's not going to talk to you. She's not even going to acknowledge you. That way if someone looks at the cameras, it will look like you just snuck in. You're on your own. You never heard of me. You never heard of my cousin. She never heard of you."

Yuri agrees with a nod of his head. "What about your cousin's money?" he asks.

"Oh, right. You put it in a bag and drop it in the trash bucket beside the door. Right before midnight. If she sees it there, she'll leave the door cracked so you can get in."

Yuri is taking mental notes. "OK, at five til, I'll drop the money, and she'll leave the door ajar."

"Yep. And then you're on your own. Got it? And if you get pinched and mention me or mention her, I will fuck you up."

Yuri doesn't doubt it. "Don't worry," he says.

Anders considers Yuri for a second. "You know why I'm doing this?" Anders asks, sipping his beer.

"The money?" Yuri answers.

"Well, yes, in part. But I also…I want to know what happened, too. I read all that stuff about you when I was a kid. I followed the whole thing. I thought that when the wall came down with Gorbachev, it would all come out. When CCCP went DOA, my first thought was, 'Finally we'll find out what really happened at the Dyatlov Pass.'"

Yuri is pleasantly surprised. "Well, thank you. And I've been trying to get into—"

Anders interrupts. "My cousin Rudolph and I talked about it one night, and we're pretty sure it was the Yeti."

"The Yeti?" Yuri asks flatly.

"Yep, the *abdominal* snowman. You're lucky he didn't rip *your* head off too."

Yuri smiles stiffly and gets up.

"Er…Well, I've got to go get ready for tonight." Yuri moves to shake hands with Anders.

Anders almost takes Yuri's hand, but then he remembers should be acting secretively. He pulls back. "Don't shake my hand, man," he whispers. "What's the matter with you? In fact, play along with this." He clears his throat. "Forget it, old man!" he says loudly. "I'm not giving you any handouts! Piss off before I beat your sorry ass! Go on. GO!!!!"

The bartender looks up from his lunch and bellows at Yuri, "What did I tell you? Bothering my customers. Shove off, grampa!"

"I'm…sorry, sir. Good day…I mean…good-bye." Yuri leaves and Anders guzzles his beer.

Later that night, Yuri takes a train and two buses to get to the government district, just around the corner from the famous Red Square in the heart of Moscow. It's

83

not snowing for a change. The air is clear, and the night is crisp. It's midnight, and the area is all but empty.

Yuri turns into an alley, checking his map with a tiny penlight. He's behind a concrete government building that occupies an entire city block. He walks slowly, trying to pinpoint his exact location. Ahead of him, he spots an exit door at the base of the giant stone edifice. Yuri thinks he's in the right place. He pulls his bag of cash from inside his coat, then notices that there's no bucket by the door.

He looks around. Further down the massive wall another set of doors opens with a metal clank. An older woman, dressed in coveralls and an apron and pushing a janitorial cart, lights a cigarette.

Yuri tentatively walks toward her.

The woman sees him. "You're late. I didn't want us to be seen together."

Yuri walks up sheepishly. "Sorry, I—"

"Doesn't matter. Anders told me who you are. You got the money?"

"Er…yes. Should I put it in the bucket?"

The woman is annoyed. "No, you can just hand it to me."

Yuri looks around. "But the cameras."

"They're down tonight. They're installing some new…something. I walked by the security window when I came in."

Yuri hands her the bag. Unconcerned, she takes out the money and counts it.

"OK, I'm going to put this smoke out and go in. Give me five minutes. The door isn't going to latch, and you can come in. Follow me from a distance. I'll go into the archives in about 45 minutes—after I mop. That door won't be latched either. You can go in after I come out with the trash. Go out that door and then this door, got it? The guard shift changes at 4:00a.m., and they walk through the main hall. You must be out by then."

"Four? That's only three hours." Yuri is upset.

"I thought you knew what you were after," the woman says.

"I do know, but there's a lot to read through. It's not as if I can just steal the files."

The woman counts the cash again and stuffs it into her apron.

"Or...can I?" Yuri asks tentatively.

The woman pitches her cigarette butt into the bucket. "I don't give a shit what you do. As far as I'm concerned, I didn't see or hear anything, and you're a famous nutball anyway. Always getting into stuff. So if they catch you stealing, that's up to you. Remember, wait for five minutes." She walks back inside and closes the door gently so that it doesn't latch. Yuri waits for five minutes and slips in.

An hour later, Yuri yawns. He sits on the floor watching the woman mop a dark, vaulted hallway. She moves on to the next room, and he follows. She throws him a glance as she unlocks the archive and pushes the cart in. Yuri's heart races as he hears her dump trash into the cart. After a few minutes, she walks out, again closing the door so that it doesn't latch. She disappears around the corner pushing her cart. He waits until all is quiet and then slinks into the archive.

Inside the darkened room, Yuri pauses. He takes out a small light with a head strap and puts it over his hat. He also has his penlight. The archive is massive, but Yuri uses a hand-drawn map to go right to a certain stack of boxes. He cuts the packing tape with a pocket-knife and starts to go through the contents of the boxes,

85

reading and taking notes, occasionally stuffing key pieces into his coat.

At the back of one of the boxes, he finds a sealed envelope. On the front it reads "Danger! Radioactive." Yuri scoffs and tears it open.

"Goddamn liars," he mumbles to himself.

Zina's aged journal, wrapped in plastic, drops into Yuri's hand. He gasps, and his hands begins to tremble. He stuffs the journal into his shirt.

He continues to sift through documents, pocketing key pieces, when suddenly he hears footsteps and male voices in the hall. Yuri scampers toward the exit and drops down. He hides behind a cabinet. Guards are talking to the cleaning woman.

"Uhh…Is there a problem, sir?" she says innocently.

"Oh, no problem, ma'am. A door sensor went off after you came through the exit door. Probably didn't latch."

"Uh…er…a door sensor?"

Yuri eases around the corner to the door in the archive. Holding his breath, he pushes it open, slowly. Gingerly, he slides out and, hugging the wall, makes his way slowly toward the exit door. He must round a corner at the end of the hall, and he will be briefly in the open before he can get to the exit. He walks silently, but one of the guards turns and spots him.

"Holy shit! There's someone in here! You. Stop!"

Yuri takes off running. He bursts out the exit door, runs around the corner, and flops down on a pile of boxes and trash. The two guards run from the building and scramble into the alley. One of them sees Yuri lying on the boxes. The other runs down the alley, looking around and calling into his radio.

The guard shakes Yuri. "Hey, pop! Hey! Wake up! You see someone come running this way?"

Yuri feigns waking up. "Whaaaaa…Lemme alone. I got no money." He pretends to doze off.

"Hey, old man! You see anyone come running this way?"

Yuri mumbles as he rolls over. "I don't know… I'm trying to sleep. There was a car here." He sits up and looks around. "Ohhhh. But now it's gone." He lies back down.

The guard shakes him again."You saw it?"

Yuri gives the performance of his life. "Nooooo. I just heard it running. Can you spare some change?"

The second guard, out of breath, runs up.

"Forget it," says the first guard. "This guy is useless. C'mon, let's circle round the block."

"Did you get a description?" the second guard asks.

"All I saw was a shadowy figure go out the door," the first guard says.

Yuri sticks out his hand. "Can you spare a few? I'm really hungry."

The flustered guard abruptly fishes in his pocket, pulls out a few bills, and sticks them in Yuri's hand. The second guard runs in the other direction, and the first guard follows.

"Sounds like they had a car waiting. The old guy saw it," the first guard yells as they run off.

"Shit. We'd better call this in."

Yuri smiles to himself. He shuffles off, his treasure safe and secure under his shirt.

Hours later, when Yuri is finally home, he sits by his stove, wrapped in blankets eating a can of heated soup by the tiny fire. He gently opens the plastic envelope, and gingerly pulls out Zina's journal.

Yuri didn't know Zina well. They'd spoken only a handful of words the entire time they'd known each other. She was shy and quiet, but when she did speak, she was obviously smart and observant.

Now, fifty years later, Yuri feels more connected to Zina than he can describe. He breathes deeply and starts to read. To his dismay, the first two-thirds of the diary are from Zina's life far before the fateful trip. The huge gaps between dates reveal that she's not a consistent diarist. Some entries simply read "boring day" or "nothing to talk about." Mostly, Zina writes about her apprehension that she will be too excited about her potential selection for the Soviet Olympic team and then will be devastated if she isn't chosen.

Finally, toward the back, Yuri finds what he is looking for.

January 28. Have to get up too early to go with the ski team up to Mt. Orton for the trip. Looking forward to just getting out in the open and skiing hard.

January 30. Slept well. Everyone is in good spirits and we're making good time. Although Alex is worried about Yuri Yudin's cough. I want to just concentrate on the skiing, but I am thinking about what Oscar said about the Olympic selection committee. That would be beyond belief. We'll see.

January 31. An eventful day and an unpleasant incident, thanks to Dyatlov. We skied well and ran into a tribe of Mansi, the indigenous, nomadic people who have lived in these mountains for hundreds of years. They were nice at first, but then got really agitated when a few of the boys tried to show them a map. An old man grabbed our new "President" Igor Dyatlov, and Dyatlov punched the poor old fellow smack in the face. I don't like him. He's an arrogant jerk and a Soviet kiss-ass. And to top it all, I got my period, two weeks early. That's never happened before.

February 1. Yuri went home sick. He has an obvious crush on L. Georgi was acting strangely this afternoon. I think maybe he caught what Yuri had. Alex thinks he's OK, maybe dehydration, but Georgi was acting so strange. What is it with people getting sick on this trip? And with that, the entries stop. Yuri flips through the diary again and again, checking all the pages, seeing if any are stuck together. But there's nothing further. Yuri sets the book down, disappointed by the lack of information. He thinks back to the days of Zina's last entries, a few hours in his life, that he has now mentally examined countless times, searching for some hint, some clue.

January 31, 1959.

In a snow-filled forest, a slope makes a natural clearing in the trees. The students ski into the clearing. Ahead of them is the camp of a group of tribesmen, the Mansi. It is a hodge-podge of tents, sod huts, and a few wooden pens with reindeer. A fire pit smolders in the center, as two children, in skins and furs, play near it. The group skis down to the Mansi herdsmen. The students are taken aback by how truly primitive the Mansi are, with their handmade animal-skin clothes and sod huts. The Mansi men have thick beards, and their faces are red and worn from constant exposure to rough weather. Two Mansi women talk as they stretch deer hide over a wooden frame. They stop work to watch the Russian students ski into their camp.

Dyatlov turns his skis sharply and stops. "Would you look at that," Dyatlov says.

Alex stops next to Dyatlov. "Not that surprising. They're Mansi. Who else?"

Lexy skis up behind them. "Whoa. Mansi. That's

pretty incredible."

The Mansi are friendly and wave to the skiers.

"Uh…Anyone speak Mansi?" Nick asks.

"Hmmm, not my specialty," Lexy mutters.

Dyatlov isn't that impressed. "They don't speak Russian? Then what are they doing here. To hell with that. We're in the Soviet Union. They should speak the tongue of Mother Russia."

Lyudmila flashes a big smile and waves to the Mansi. "Hello, hello. How are you?"

The Mansi tribe is led by a young and imposing chief known as Surek. He's muscular and tall, with a weathered face that is strong and solid. His eyes are almost black and deeply set. He smiles as he greets the students. They all shake hands.

Zina is delighted. "This is amazing," she says.

Yuri is impressed too. "It's unbelievable. We used to read about these people in geography."

"Should I take some pictures?" Georgi smiles and reaches for his camera.

Alex toys with Georgi. "I don't know. Some primitive cultures think cameras steal their souls. You wouldn't want them to go berserk and scalp us."

Georgi gets nervous and lowers his camera. "Wh-what are you talking about?"

Lexy laughs at Georgi and smiles at the gathering herdsmen. "He's pulling your chain, Georgi."

Zina gives Alex a friendly jab in the ribs.

Georgi scoffs and snaps a couple of photos. "Come now, boys. Be respectful. Big smiles, everyone."

Everyone greets each other.

"Hello, Hello. Nice to meet you," Doreshenko says. "They can't understand a word I'm saying, can they?"

"Hello. Thank you for letting us pass—and not scalping us," Nick says.

"Shhhh! Nick, be nice!" Zina says.

"Not too bad on the Mansi female either. Look at her, Lexy." Nick motions to Lexy. The two men stare at a young Mansi girl, both beautiful and shy.

Lexy whispers, "You aren't kidding. Boy, I wish I spoke Mansi."

"No need, my friend. I speak the international language of lovvvve," Nick replies.

Lyudmila isn't amused with their antics. "You guys, grow up."

A little Mansi girl runs up and gives a hard, cookie like biscuit to Lyudmila.

"Oh, well, thank you," Lyudmila says loudly and clearly.

The little girl talks in Mansi and points to her mouth. Lyudmila understands. She takes a bite and smiles. Lyudmila then takes out a package of crackers and gives one to the little girl.

"And here. What about you?" Other children, seeing Lyudmila hand out crackers, crowd around her. "There you go. Oh, and you want one? Well, here you are. Enjoy."

Lyudmila is tickled with the encounter. She gives crackers to all of them. The children talk and laugh as they enjoy the new food.

Yuri watches Lyudmila and admires her. He wants to say something, but it's all he can do to stifle his nagging cough.

"Awww, these kids are just terrific," says Doroshenko.

Surek signals to a few tribeswomen, who promptly give the skiers strips of dried reindeer meat.

Doreshenko takes a few strips. "Hey, that stuff looks pretty good."

"We can't just take their food. Let's trade," Georgi says.

Everyone fishes out stuff to trade for the meat: a pencil and paper, a comb, an apple, a small loaf of bread, a can of beans, matches, and an extra ski hat.

Dyatlov stands off to one side. He is angry about anything that slows their journey.

The Mansi are grateful for the exchange.

Doroshenko prods Nick. "Hey, Nick, show him your map. Make sure we are where we think we are."

"Oh, that's a good idea," Georgi says.

Nick takes out his map and shows it to Surek and two other men. "Um...I'm sorry, but could you take a look at this?"

Dyatlov is growing more impatient. "I don't think we need to check your map work with these... people. They don't even use maps."

Surek and the other men pore over the map.

Alex is getting tired of Dyatlov's constant push. "Well, I'd just like to make sure. If you don't mind." He talks to the Mansi in a clear, loud voice, pointing out their route on the map. "We started here. Then we skied through here. Are we here? Is this here?"

The Mansi study the map. They nod to each other and point to the spot on the map. They understand. Surek spots the group's intended route traced in red pencil on the map. He tries to get the students to explain, but they can't understand him.

"Damn, Alex. Not bad. I'll never doubt you again." Doroshenko is impressed.

"I told you, I've got a system. You can never get lost with the right maps."

Surek points to the red line, speaking fast in Mansi. He taps the red pencil line on the map.

Doroshenko tries to explain. "Yes, that's our trip. We're going to circle up around here, cross over to this side, go up Mt. Orton, and then come back to Vizhai."

Surek and the other Mansi men talk and grow concerned. Two other Mansi men join the discussion. They all talk about the map. Surek points toward the mountain. He talks and gestures, but the team doesn't understand.

"What's wrong?" Nick asks.

"I think he's telling us a story or something." Doroshenko isn't sure.

Nick talks loudly to the Mansi. "Yes, thank you. That's fascinating."

The whole village buzzes as the Mansi men grow agitated. Surek taps on the map fervently. The mood has suddenly turned.

"What does he mean?" Zina asks.

Dyatlov is exasperated at all the wasted time. "Who cares? We're burning what little daylight we have left. Let's go. You're an accurate navigator. Great. So let's get going!"

Zina is concerned. "Hang on a minute. It's as if they don't want us to go."

The villagers are excited and appear to be worried. These foreigners are talking about the mountain. Some villagers seem frantic. A mother steps in and whisks all the children into a hut.

"Look, let's just go. We're upsetting them." Zina says.

Surek insistently presses the team, but no one can understand. Surek tries to explain. He looks around and finally wipes his finger on a burnt log. He draws a big black smudge on the map.

"Hey, I need that," Nick exclaims, trying to grab the map back.

"This is a little much; did he just put a spell on the map?" Rusty laughs at the awkward confusion.

Dyatlov skis into the group and grabs the map from Surek. He throws it back to Nick.

"This is ridiculous. Let's go. I don't have time for some babbling caveman."

"Dyatlov, calm down." Lyudmila steps in.

An old tribesman is particularly riled up and babbles incoherently. He's in a panic as he struggles to communicate to the team.

Doroshenko tries to calm him. "I'm sorry. I don't understand you."

Dyatlov shakes his head and starts to ski off. "I'm going. Good-bye. This is asinine, really."

The old man runs beside Dyatlov, ranting and yelling, desperately trying to make Dyatlov understand his warning. He grabs Dyatlov's arm just as Dyatlov picks up speed. Without hesitating, Dyatlov punches the old man square in the jaw. The old man drops into the snow. Lyudmila and Zina move to help him up.

"What the hell!" Zina snaps. "You're such an ass, Dyatlov."

Now the whole tribe bristles with anger. They yell at the group. The students don't understand the words, but they clearly get the meaning. Two of the Mansi men pull out skinning knives. Surek takes command and orders everyone to calm down. The students are in a jumble as they try to back up with skis on.

"Great. Now they *are* going to scalp us," Doroshenko says nervously.

"Maybe we should just get going," says Yuri.

"The damage is done." He is already turning around. The group is trying to leave as respectfully as they can.

"Yes, I think that leaving be wise," Rusty adds.

"We're just making the situation worse by staying," Alex says.

The team silently skis out of the camp. Yuri looks at all the pairs of dark eyes fixed on him as they leave.

"We're sorry, so sorry," Lyudmila says. She is troubled and talks to the tribe even though she knows they don't understand her. "So sorry. Please don't judge all of us because of...well, I mean...I'm sorry."

The team skis out of camp and into the snow-covered trees. The Mansi are still agitated. Two women inspect the old man, who seems fine. Others gather up the items they received from the students and toss them into the fire. Several women begin to cry and wail. It's a very bad omen for the Mansi. Surek is concerned as he watches the skiers disappear among the trees.

The next morning, the rising sun fills the small valley where the team camps. The skiers are taking down the tents, finishing their food, and packing. Yuri poses while Georgi takes a picture of him with Zina and Lyudmila. As the shutter clicks, Yuri has a violent coughing attack. Doroshenko and Rusty glance at each other with concern as Yuri continues to cough.

Nearby, Dyatlov, packed and ready, sits on a downed tree, eating the dried Mansi reindeer meat. Dyatlov chews on a strip of the meat. "This meat is really good and fresh," he says.

"Yeah, too bad you had to punch the poor man who gave it to us," Alex says as he rolls up his sleeping bag.

"It's true. You're a real ambassador of friendship,

Dyatlov," Zina quips.

"He grabbed me. No one grabs me unless I want to be grabbed," Dyatlov says.

"It seemed pretty obvious that they didn't want us to keep going," Rusty says as he rinses out his coffee cup and puts it in his pack.

"Witchcraft. They aren't even Soviet citizens. They're morons," Dyatlov decides.

Yuri has another coughing fit. "You sound like shit, Yudin." Dyatlov says.

"It's fine. I'm fine, I'm telling you," Yuri insists.

Lyudmila sits next to Yuri and feels his forehead. "How do you feel, Yuri?"

Yuri tries to talk but starts coughing again.

Zina is worried too. "Oh, Yuri, that can't be good."

"Sounds real bad," Dyatlov says. "Alex, you're a med student. What do you think?"

Alex doesn't want to get into it but has no choice. He squats down and looks at Yuri closely. "Uh... Yeah, you look like a carp, Yudin."

Dyatlov stands up and makes a theatrical proclamation. "That's it. I think we're going to have to cut the carp loose. Sorry, Yudin, I can't risk you making everyone sick."

"Now hang on, Dyatlov." Doroshenko stands up.

"Yeah, I think it's up to Yuri," Rusty agrees.

"What about it, Yudin?" Nick asks. "You know what we're going up against. Are you up for it? Twenty kilometers a day?"

Dyatlov can't be quiet. "Twenty? I didn't think we were dragging grannies along. I was thinking thirty."

"I feel fine, really. It just sounds bad." Yuri gets up, rolls up his sleeping bag, and ties it to his pack.

Lyudmila sits down next to Yuri. "It does sound bad, really bad. Yuri, do you think you're up to it?"

"Uh…I guess…I mean…I don't know. Yes, I am. Uh...Bloody hell. I'm sorry."

She puts her arm around him. "Don't be sorry, but I think you're pretty sick."

"Don't take this too hard, Yudin," Dyatlov adds, "but I can't put the team in jeopardy. What if you get us all sick? You need to be 100 percent for a trip like this."

"Hey, Dyatlov," Yuri snaps. "You made your point, OK? I'm heading back. Give it a rest, will you?"

"Don't be sore, buddy, another time."

Yuri stands up, puts on his pack, and steps into his skis. "Well then, I guess I shouldn't linger. If I've got to go down in one day."

One by one, the team says good-bye to Yuri—with a pat on the head or a handshake.

Lexy pats him on the shoulder. "Sorry, brother."

Rusty shakes Yuri's hand and whispers, "You're going to save yourself a lot of pain."

The students make final adjustments to their gear and put on their hats and gloves.

Yuri stands near Lyudmila as she finishes putting on her skis. "Hey, take it easy up there. Don't let him drive you to the brink," he tells her.

"I'll be OK. I think we can mutiny if necessary."

"OK…well…I'm off then." Yuri lingers, hoping perhaps Lyudmila might offer to come with him.

She senses something but doesn't get it. She cocks her head and gives Yuri a puzzled look. "You OK?"

"I'm still on my feet. That's something. And it's just a little downhill back to the train."

She holds his arm. "It's still all day, Yuri, even if

you go fast. So, please, take care."

"Lyudy," Zina calls, "can you give me a hand with these damn straps?" Zina struggles with her pack.

"You bet."

There's an awkward pause, and Lyudy finally gives Yuri a friendly hug. Yuri turns and skis down the hill without looking back.

Nick watches him disappear into the trees. "Poor Yuri. That's too bad."

"To hell with Yuri Yudin," Dyatlov proclaims. "He's slower than an ox. Besides, he'd slow Lyudmila down, hanging on her the way he does. He's like a puppy."

Lyudmila doesn't hesitate. "And you're like a shitty sewer rat, Dyatlov, sniffing around where you shouldn't."

The others howl at the dig, but Dyatlov bristles at being made the butt of a joke. "Whoa. Tsk, tsk. Soooo, what else you can do with that mouth?"

The group groans collectively.

Lyudmila comes right back. "Bite your shitty little rat head off, that's what I could do."

The others roar with laughter. Dyatlov is flustered and annoyed. "OK, OK, you're saucy. We get it. Now," he says in an effort to change the subject, "Let's get this going. The day is burning."

"Yeah, and so are your ears!" Nick throws in one last dig and skis off. The group roars with laughter as they set off into the morning.

Beyond the trees, it's a bright, clear, and cold. They are alone in the mountains, and each feels a rush of exhilaration as they ski through pristine valleys and over spectacular ridges. They all revel in the perfection of the moment, the elements coming together, the ability to do what very few others can do. The tracks of their skis are the only sign of humans for as far as the eye can see. As they drop into a snow-filled valley, Doroshenko gives an enthusiastic yell that echoes into the canyon. One by one, as they ski into the pass, they give their own versions of the war cry. They howl and laugh. They make great time, and suddenly all of the pain is unquestionably worth it. The group works hard and skis well. They're having fun, hiking up hills and skiing down the other side. They're all in good form. They ski all day and into the late afternoon.

As evening sets in, they stop for the night. In a clearing, thickly surrounded by trees, they find a good spot. The sun sets behind the mountains as they put up their three tents, and Dyatlov gets started on a fire pit.

An hour later, they've eaten, and the fire is roaring. Lexy plays a harmonica, and Nick sings a bawdy song. A flask of vodka goes around, and everybody is feeling happy and relaxed—except Dyatlov, who chops wood with vigor.

Rusty watches Dyatlov and finally yells at him, "Dyatlov! For shit's sake, relax for one second, will you? That fire is going to burn all night!"

"That's the idea," Dyatlov says as he chops.

"It's not safe. You'll burn down the forest," Zina says with a giggle and a burp.

"Not likely," Dyatlov responds.

Like the others, Lexy is feeling no pain. He calls to Dyatlov, "Relax, Dyatlov. For goodness sake, have a drink. Get into the spirit."

Dyatlov continues to chop. "Drink clouds the brain. It's bad for the body."

Nick salutes Dyatlov and takes a big swig. "Ha! That's the point, you maniac."

"What I think our intrepid leader is saying is that he," Alex says in a loud whisper, "can't hold his liquor."

"Is that what he's saying?" Nick plays along. "Igor Dyatlov, how do you respond to that?"

Dyatlov is breathing hard and grips his hatchet. "How do I respond to that?" Dyatlov walks over to Rusty and stands over him. The group collectively holds their breath. Dyatlov snatches the flask out of Rusty's hand. He stands, breathing heavily, silhouetted by the roaring fire behind him. From the silver flask, he takes a huge swallow.

"Nostrovia!" He yells. They all erupt in laughter.

"Attaboy, Dyatlov!" Doroshenko yells. "Lexy, play us some music. Dyatlov, show us how well Russians dance!"

Dyatlov is happy to oblige. "Oh, I'm such a good dancer, You don't deserve it, Give me another drink first!" Lexy plays a tune, and Dyatlov jumps around to the music in front of the roaring fire. The men and women, in the middle of nowhere, laugh, sing, and talk under a black sky, splattered with innumerable stars.

Hours later, all have crawled into their respective tents and collapsed into deep sleep. The fire has burned down to a wide bed of glowing, red coals. Lyudmila and Zina are asleep in one small tent across the fire pit from Rusty, Nick, and Alex in their tent. Dyatlov and the three other men are in the largest tent around the fire. The night is moonless. The faint glow of fire paints the snow with a dim, orange light.

Silently, a dark shape carefully crosses in front of the embers that pulse and glow. Dyatlov, wearing just his long underwear and socks, slowly unties the flap of the women's tent and slides inside. He silently and purposefully slides in behind Lyudmila, who is sleeping soundly. He slowly snuggles up behind her and gets under her sleeping bag. He studies her in the faint light and then abruptly starts to suck on her neck and clumsily rub her breasts.

After a day of skiing and a night of drinking, Lyudmila is in a deep sleep. She slowly starts to come around. "Uh…urghh…ummmm…"

Dyatlov whispers in her ear. "C'mon, Lyudy, you don't think I know what they say? I'll show you. I'll put it to you good. You'll be sore for a month when I'm done with you."

Lyudmila forces herself to come to. She's confused and disoriented.

Dyatlov climbs on top of her. "Oh, my blonde beauty. Just relax."

Lyudmila struggles to consciousness. "What? No! Wait! Stop! Stop! What are you doing? Stop it!"

Rusty staggers out of his tent to take a drunken piss. He's groggy and still half drunk. He hears the commotion and looks into the tent, confused.

Zina wakes up as well. She turns on her flashlight.

"What's going on?" yells Rusty as he grabs Dyatlov by the ankle and pulls him off Lyudmila. "Dyatlov? What in the hell are you doing?"

"That asshole was all over me!" Lyudmila yells.

Nick pokes his head into the tent. Within seconds everyone is awake.

"Dyatlov, what are you doing?" asks Nick. "This isn't even your tent. What was he doing?"

Dyatlov feigns confusion and plays drunker than he is. "Er…uhhh…What? What are you talking about? This is my tent, damn it!" he yells.

"No, it isn't," says Nick. "Look around you."

Lexy and Alex poke their heads into the tent. "What's wrong? We heard yelling."

Everyone is up, disoriented and confused.

"Dyatlov. He was all over me. I…I…"

Dyatlov plays up the drunken act. "I was just out taking a piss, and then I was trying to go to bed, but she was in my sleeping bag."

Alex and Lexy pull Dyatlov out of the tent. Nick pushes Dyatlov back to his own tent.

"Well, that proves it, Dyatlov," says Nick. "You can't hold your booze. Wrong tent, pal. Let's go."

Alex and Nick check on Lyudmila, who just wants to go back to sleep. Eventually, all is calm, and everyone returns to bed.

"Look at that. Georgi didn't even wake up. Bum!" Doroshenko says.

Back inside the women's tent, Zina is half awake, still confused by the whole thing. She turns off her flashlight. The tent goes dark except for the orange glow shining through the flaps.

"What an ass! You OK, Lyudy?"

"I'm fine. It's fine. Just go back to sleep."

Zina starts to fall back to sleep. "That guy. We need a bear trap outside. Then maybe we could get some sleep."

"No kidding. Rotten little pecker. All right, good night."

Silence returns, but Lyudmila can't sleep. She stares at the tent door, watching the firelight flicker on the tent ceiling. There is no breeze, no noise, except the crackling of the embers and the soft snoring of a couple of the men. The silence rushes in Lyudmila's mind, and she has no choice but to listen to the faint sounds all night.

The next morning is again clear and bright but cold. Everyone is stretching, pulling their gear together, finishing coffees, and packing.

Lyudmila brushes her teeth next to a small pail of water attached to a tree. Zina walks over and dips her toothbrush in.

"What was going on last night?"

"You got me," Lyudmila says quietly.

"He didn't seem that drunk when we all went to bed," Zina says.

"He wasn't that drunk. This will be my last outing with Igor Dyatlov."

"No kidding. He didn't—?"

"No. Are you kidding? I don't know what he felt, but I felt something poking the back of my knee, and he was sucking on my neck—like a leech."

"Ugh! That *is* disgusting." Zina makes a face.

They laugh apprehensively.

"The worst part is, I didn't get a wink of sleep."

Across the campsite, Alex stands away from the rest as everyone prepares to leave. He calls to Dyatlov. "Hey, Dyatlov, come here. I've got a good idea on traversing this valley."

Alex walks through the trees away from the group. Dyatlov follows and stands looking out over the small valley.

"Where? Over there? Yeah, that might work. Right down through there. You want to take point today, Alex?"

"Sure. But first—" Alex takes his ski pole and smacks Dyatlov over the head with it. Dyatlov falls to the snow, clutching his forehead.

"Ahhhh, shit. What the—? Have you lost your goddamn mind?"

"You had a bee on your head," Alex says casually.

"Whaaaat?" Dyatlov is reeling.

Alex picks up his bent ski pole and points at Dyatlov with it. "Shut your little mouth. We all put up with your bullshit because you're a good mountain man, and you've got a lot of energy, and were dedicated to the club and each other."

"I'm bleeding, you prick." Dyatlov clutches his forehead.

"Don't you get up, or I'll do it again. You know, I'm going to be a flight surgeon after school, so It's not a big deal to have to put up with an asshole like you. The military will be filled with them, so it's good practice for me."

"I'm going to—" Dyatlov tries to threaten Alex.

"Here's how it's going to play out. If you bother Lyudy or Zina or anyone else, beyond running that shit filled mouth—"

Dyatlov scoffs at Alex. "Oh, please. What the hell are you going to do? Huh? This is my trip. This is my deal."

"All of us have been in this club longer than you. As for club president, I didn't want you. So I don't give a shit how many push-ups you can do. You try and rape anyone again, and I will put this ski pole in your eye."

"This is ridiculous. I was sleep walking."

"Save it. Just save it. It's insulting that you think I'd fall for that crap." Alex straightens his ski pole. "See you on the trail, pal. Better get going. The day is burning away." Alex stomps off and back to his gear.

Dyatlov pulls his hat down to cover the blow on his forehead and rejoins the team.

Dyatlov is shaky and aching, but no one seems to notice as he struggles through the morning—trying to ski with a pounding knot on his forehead. The team makes good progress through the day and stops briefly for lunch. Dyatlov's head pounds, but he starts to recover as they ski on. They cross out of the trees and onto the open landscape. It's sunny and strangely quiet out in the open. The only sounds are of the students chatting and of the skis moving back and forth across the snow.

"You don't have all the details," Doroshenko says. He and Lexy are in a heated conversation as they ski along.

"I say it's a concern. That's all. The Americans are going to turn Alaska and Hawaii into states, probably this year or the next. Do you know how many square kilometers of land that is?" Lexy says.

"Yeah, but it's not like they invaded those places. They've had them forever. It's like a formality, mostly," Doroshenko argues.

Lexy pants and puffs as they slog uphill. "I know you love Hollywood and New York, but I can't say I trust them."

"Lexy, let's just say you don't have all the facts. You can't believe everything that is written," Doroshenko says.

Rusty skis alongside Nick and Zina. They all breathe heavily as they slog up a hill.

"What the hell did we do this for, again? Rusty asks. "I should have stayed home—or bailed out with Yuri. I slept like shit. I've been having the most disturbing dreams lately."

"Me too," Lexy says as he skis up to the group. "Every night. It's so weird."

"Thanks to lover boy up there, I didn't get a

wink. But what did you dream?" Lyudmila asks.

"I don't remember, but I remember being so scared, absolutely terrified. When I woke up, I was so relieved to know it was a dream, whatever it was," Lexy recalls.

"I'm guessing it's because of Nick's gas. We're sleeping in a cloud of it, and it's suffocating us!" Alex says.

"Wait, I'm not even in the same tent as Nick, and I had weird dreams,too," Zina says.

"That's how potent it is!"

They all laugh and continue their slog.

Nick has been following the conversation. "That is so funny—and mature, too," Nick gripes.

"Why do I do this to myself?" Rusty pants.

"It's good for you! I love it, and you do too—or you wouldn't keep doing it," Zina tells Rusty as she pushes past him.

"The brain does that. You quickly forget the highs and lows," Alex explains in a medical-student fashion. "You forget the pain and just remember the fun parts—the great views, the downhill but not the up. That's why you can't ever remember sex. It's just too good. It always feels way better than you can ever re-member. Memory is great for recording events but not necessarily the feeling of an event. That isn't as easily recorded."

"That seems true. Because I had somehow com-pletely forgotten what a prick Dyatlov could be." Nick nods toward Dyatlov far up ahead.

Rusty is beat, and so is Lyudmila. Neither of them slept well. "OK, I'm ready to take a breather. Let's stop and rest a second," Rusty pants.

"I think Georgi beat you to it," says Lyudmila.

"Look." Georgi has stopped and is staring off into the distant trees, well behind the team.

"Dyatlov is going to be pissed if we stop," Doroskenko warns.

"Screw him!" says Rusty. "We're not in the miliary yet. Hey, Alex! Alex! Stop for a second."

Ahead, the rest of the group is slogging up a slope single file. They all stop. Dyatlov turns, immediately irritated.

"What's going on? What's up with Georgi?" Dyatlov skis past the others down to Georgi. "What the hell? Damn it! If we're not going to train seriously, what is the damn point?"

Rusty, Zina, and Nick join Dyatlov and Georgi. Georgi stands transfixed, his eyes on the tree line.

Nick skis up and calls to Georgi. "Georgi! What's going on? Georgi? Georgi?"

Georgi slowly snaps out of it. The others crowd around, concerned. Georgi talks softly, and his words drift off. "I saw something. I saw something in the trees. I should have taken a picture..."

"What? Georgi, what did you say?" Zina asks.

"What's going on? Georgi, why are you stopping?" Doroshenko skis up to the group.

Dyatlov is annoyed. "Georgi,what the hell? Let's go. Why are you always dead last?"

Georgi lifts his arm and slowly points to the tree line. "I saw something. I saw someone in the...in the trees. It was...moving."

"What? Someone? Georgi, did you say someone? Where exactly?" Nick scans the horizon with his binoculars, trying to see where Georgi points.

"It was big. It was a shape. I thought it was moving, but then I thought maybe it was just something in my eye."

They all exchange perplexed and concerned glances.

"What? Georgi, are you feeling OK? That doesn't make any sense," says Alex.

"Was it a bear? Could it have been a big black bear or something?" Lexy asks.

"I don't know. It's hard to describe. It…confused my eyes…at first. It was moving. but then I thought I saw fire."

Nick studies the tree line. "Couldn't have been fire, Georgi. There's no smoke. Can't have fire without smoke."

They are bewildered. Georgi seems to be in a trance, as if he's sleepwalking.

"What the shit, Georgi? What the hell are you talking about?" Dyatlov demands.

Alex pulls out his canteen. He gives Georgi a drink. "C'mon, buddy, take a drink of this. You might be getting dehydrated. We went hard all day yesterday, drank booze last night. How much water have you had?"

"What was it, Georgi? What did you see?" asks Zina.

"Maybe…maybe nothing. Maybe it was just something in my eye. But for a second it felt like it was someone. It was as if someone was there, and I knew it, and they knew I was here and—"

Zina tries to make firm eye contact with Georgi. "Georgi, look at me. Do you want to go on? Are you all right?"

Lyudmila takes off her glove and touches his forehead under his hat. "Doesn't seem like he has a fever."

"You might have caught whatever Yuri had, you guys were in the same tent the first night," says Zina.

"You sound strange," Lexy says.

Georgi blinks and looks around. He rubs his eyes. "I'm fine, really."

The group is concerned, except for Dyatlov. "Oh, such bullshit. What the hell? Are we going to do this or what? Georgi, do you want to continue, or are you too sick? Yes or no?"

"No, I'm fine. I'm not sure what I saw. Maybe it was a brain trick or something," Georgi mutters.

"Fine. It was a brain trick. Now can we go?"

Alex is looking at Georgi's eyes and puts his hand on Georgi's forehead as well. "Jesus, Dyatlov, I want to know if he's OK. If he gets sick, then every meter we go is just another meter we're going to have to retrace."

"Damn it! He said he's fine. Let's just keep going. And if he's sick, he can go back. I'm not retracing anything. I'm going on just like we planned. That's the point!"

"What *is* the point, Dyatlov?" Doroshenko barks.

"To do this. To beat the outdoors. Are we going to have a big philosophical discussion here? We're Russians. We're the strongest people on earth, and I hold that title in high regard!" Dyatlov turns and starts back up the slope.

Alex calls up to him. "Boy, Dyatlov, you have a way of really taking the fun out of it. That's another talent you excel at."

Dyatlov is exasperated. His head still throbs. "Uh...OK, fine. We've been climbing. When we get to the top of that ridge, it's going to be downhill into that valley. C'mon. First person down to the bottom wins a case of pilsner on me!" Dyatlov turns and takes off.

Doroshenko takes a sip from his canteen. He passes it around. "We'd better go. He'll be in Mongolia before night fall. Georgi, are you sure?"

"Yes, let's go." Georgi gives a thumbs-up.

The team crests the hill and drops into a smooth, perfect valley. The sun is out, and, in spite of everything, they begin to actually have fun again, whizzing down the mountain, slaloming through the trees, and laughing—with Dyatlov always racing ahead.

A couple of hours later, Dyatlov waits in a clearing.

Nick skis up and stops with a big spray of snow. He gasps for breath. "Ha! Now that was a good run. Woooooo!"

One by one, the others ski in. Dyatlov checks his watch, timing everyone. They're all exhilarated and drink from canteens, catching their breath.

"That was a great run, just great!" Doroshenko exclaims.

"Hell, yes!" Lexy agrees.

Zina drinks some water and catches her breath. "Wooweeee, that was good."

"I was in it. I was in that place where you're just glued to the trail! Oh, you'd better believe there's nothing like that!" Rusty adds.

Dyatlov is ready to go again. "C'mon! Let's keep the energy going! Up the mountain. We can make camp beyond that ridge. Look, the weather is perfect! Rested long enough? Who's with me?" Dyatlov takes off up a slope between trees. The rest of the team can't believe it.

"Uh…OK, first one to strangle Dyatlov isn't the rotten egg!" Lexy offers.

"Forget it. I'm at least taking a fiver. Sorry," says Nick as he drops into the snow. The rest follow suit, flopping into a snowdrift.

"It's an ass mutiny," Alex notes and plops down. "Someone has got to have a flask."

Lexy reaches into his coat. "Ta-da!"

They all sit back.

Dyatlov skis back over. "Owwwww! What now? Let's not stop. We've got our momentum up. Are we going to take naps next? C'mon. Daylight is burning."

Everyone groans, Nick tosses a wad of snow at Dyatlov. "Dyatlov, relax for one second, will you? We just want to rest. Have you even, for one second, noticed this beautiful country around us?"

Dyatlov tries to switch gears. He breathes deeply and thinks. "I can relax. Really. I can do anything I put my mind to." He takes off his skis and walks around. "I know you guys think I'm too...energetic, but years ago, I read a quote by this solider, and he said, 'One day, everyone is going to either sit down, lie down, or fall down, and they'll never get up again, ever.'"

Everyone is silent. They throw each other quizzical glances.

"I don't know why, but it always stuck in my mind, and it motivates me."

Once again, the group is taken aback by Dyatlov's strange candidness.

Lyudmila offers an alternate perspective. "That's a great quote, Dyatlov, but maybe it wasn't meant to be taken so literally. I mean, you can sit down and still be doing things. You don't always have to be 'on the move.' Look around. Look at this beautiful landscape. We're the only people on earth to see this exact view. There's no harm in just sitting and taking it in. You don't always have to compete to live."

Dyatlov paces and looks around, trying too hard to take Lyudmila's advice. "Wow, you're right. This is a beautiful spot, for sure. I love it. And that was a great run, for everyone." He paces back and forth. He walks over to a bare tree. There's a branch that he can just reach. He looks up at the tree limb, tugs on it, and unconsciously starts doing pull-ups.

"Yep, absolutely beautiful, this country of ours." Dyatlov continues doing pull-ups. "And look at the weather right now. Not a cloud in the sky. Perfect for cross-country trailblazing. Wow! Look at the color."

The rest just laugh out loud at one-dimensional Dyatlov.

"Dyatlov, you are soooo transparent," Alex laughs. "C'mon. Give us ten more chin-ups. Go! All right, everyone, Commander Dyatlov is through taking in the beautiful scenery, and we have orders to assault that hill. Now fall out, men—and women." Everyone giggles salutes and makes wise cracks.

"Aye, aye, sir!" Zina barks in a man's voice.

They all get to their feet, position their skis, and find another reserve of energy.

As they press on into the day, the clouds quietly choke out the setting sun, and the wind picks up.

Ten kilometers away, down in the forest, twilight falls where the Mansi have tucked a new camp into a stand of tall pine trees. A large fire burns in the center. The Mansi tents circle the campsite, their herd of reindeer in rope pens. The Mansi haven't begun to build sod huts or permanent animal pens because they aren't convinced they've gone far enough away from the recent incident.

A few of the tribesmen sit around the fire cooking and quietly talking. The wind howls in the trees above, but the camp is protected in the thick forest. The men around the fire still speak cautiously of the recent events and are startled when Surek staggers out of his tent and drops to his knees. He swoons and wretches and wipes snow on his sweating face. The men sitting around the fire jump up. Surek's wife follows him out of his tent.

"Surek, are you OK? Surek, what's wrong?" his wife asks, her voice trembling with fear.

"Surek, what's wrong? What's the matter?" another man asks.

"Those kids. Those arrogant Soviet children. They're moving onto the mountain. We must get them off that mountain. We must go. Now."

"Now?" The men are hesitant and look at each other with fear.

"Now. Get the men. Get the snowshoes. And make torches. We must go." Surek is shaky but stands up.

"Are you...are you sure?" his wife asks.

"I have seen it. It overtook me as I slept, and I've seen it. We have to go. *Now!*"

On the mountain, the weather is showing its teeth. In the deepening twilight, a howling storm, a near white-out blizzard blasts the students as they trudge along.

Lyudmila can barely see who is in front of her, as she nervously sings to herself. "When I was two, I had a blue shoe. When I was three, I had a pet flea. When I was four, I could open a door. When I was fi—" She stops and looks back. Now she can't see who is behind her. She looks forward. She can't see who is in front of her. She is disoriented and spins around in the snow. Her world is a gray, moving sea of air and snow, and the roaring wind howls into her ears. Only her skis and her hands, digging in with the ski poles, seem real and solid in this swirling world of white. She can see the tracks of whoever is in front of her, and she mechanically and obediently follows them.

Then something moves, under the snow, just at the edge of her vision. She can't be sure. She shakes it off. Snow pelts her face, and she wipes her goggles. She sees nothing, but she replays the memory in her mind. It was like a body slowly rolling over under a thick blanket, and then it was gone. Logically, it could have been a trick of the light, maybe a swirl of air whipping the surface of the snow. Logically, that was it. But then why is she suddenly so terrified? Why is she so panicked? And why had she just slightly urinated herself?

She spins around and starts to sweat. Georgi's earlier sighting lurks in her mind. In the blinding show, under her layers of clothing, she sweats profusely. She slogs forward. Something catches her eye again through the snow, but it's gone as quickly as she can focus on it. She seals her eyes shut and thinks of what Georgi said, what he thought he saw.

She can feel it. She can feel that someone, a stranger, is somehow watching her, just like Georgi said. She has never been so sure of a feeling in her life. Something is watching her.

Out of the whiteness, Zina almost falls on top of Lyudmila. The two women right each other and start calling for Doroshenko. They both call out. "Doroshenko, we have to stop!"

Doroshenko relays the message to Dyatlov in

front of him. "Dyatlov, they're yelling for us, I think. We have to stop."

"We have to stop. I can't see. I can't feel my hands," Zina shouts.

"We need to camp," Doroshenko yells over the howling wind.

One by one, the rest of the group comes ahead, crowding around Lyudmila and Zina. Doroshenko and Dyatlov come back down the line.

Rusty and Lexy agree. "She's right," says Rusty. "Let's ski back down to the trees!"

The storm pummels the group. The wind howls. They can barely hear one another.

"What?" Lexy yells.

"We've got to make camp," says Rusty. "Head back down to the trees before it gets totally dark!"

"No, let's stop here. Let's set up a tent, here," Dyatlov yells.

"What? Why?" asks Rusty. "The forest is just back there. The tree line is just back there."

"No! Didn't you hear Zina? She can't feel her hands. We'll camp here. It would be too dark by the time we got down there."

"That doesn't make sense," Alex disagrees. "Let's get out of the wind. And since when do you care if someone can't feel their hands?"

"What?" Dyatlov can't hear over the wind.

"I agree with Dyatlov. Let's set up the big tent and ride this out," Lexy yells.

"He's right," says Doroshenko. "We could be in the tent already. C'mon. Everyone help. Get the ropes. Move, move!"

The group struggles to set up their largest tent in the driving wind. The work is agonizingly slow. Everyone is numb with cold. They move in slow motion. Finally the tent is up, and they pile inside.

The Mansi tribesmen, dressed in huge fur-lined skins, with snowshoes and torches, move through the forest. The wind sways the huge trees, and large chunks of snow drop from shattered tree limbs, as the trees creak and bend in the torturing wind.

The Mansi walk through the forest for hours. Finally the trees thin out. They leave the forest and walk out onto the open plain in the foothills of the mountains. Out in the open, the weather abruptly changes, and the night is suddenly calm. Only the sounds of tree limbs behind them, still reeling from the blast, break and snap as huge trunks creak and fall with muffled thuds to the forest floor.

The Mansi stop at the edge of the forest and look up into the bare foothills and the mountains beyond, hidden in a blanket of clouds.

"Look! What is that?"

One man points, but everyone can easily see the flickering orange lights that swirl in the sky and fly through the clouds. The clouds glow and twist as the lights swirl and pass through them, distorting the thick clouds and pulling out ribbons of vapor as they move. Strange sounds rumble through the valley as half of the Mansi tribesmen drop to their knees Others huddle behind a log.

One of the men, his eyes wide open, peers from behind the log. He doesn't take his eyes off the orbs. He whispers to Surek, who stands motionless. "Surek, what is it? Is that of the Russians or of the Gods?"

Surek doesn't know what to think. He cannot believe his eyes, but he can feel the urgency of finding the skiers. The mountain is pulling him up.

Without warning, a wall of white wind and fog blows down the mountain at the speed of a freight train. The tribe is instantly and viciously blasted as the torrent of wind and snow explodes on them. Surek and his men fight to stay on their feet. The strange storm is too strong, enveloping the men in a complete whiteout. Their torches are instantly snuffed by the driving wind.

"This is bad. This is a sign. We can't do this," a tribesmen yells to rest.

"No, we...we need to get—" Surek senses the danger the students are in and wants to continue.

One of his men is on the verge of panic. "Surek! We can't go on. We can't!"

The snow blasts them. Surek has never felt anything like it. "You're right. Everyone back. We can't go out in this. Everyone back!"

The Mansi retreat into the protection of the forest and work their way back to their encampment, beaten and battered, with frostbitten noses and ears. Beyond the trees and up on the mountain, the roaring storm whites out the area completely.

Moscow 2009.

It is a calm night. Heavy clouds hang over the city, but it's not snowing. Everywhere, snow is turning to slush. Yuri wipes sauce off his beard as he walks along, eating a gooey, cheap sandwich. He shuffles through the mushy snow and crosses a street into a poor neighborhood that continues for blocks. Yuri checks the address—the precious address, another treasure he liberated from the archives.

He enters one of the huge identical buildings and walks through the drab, simple lobby. A laundry room is attached, and a few people watch TV as washers and dryers hum away. Yuri pokes around and finds the tiny elevator—out of order. Nearby is a flight of stairs, and he climbs to the second floor.

Blaring rock music and a crying baby echo through the building as Yuri stands on the small landing, which is stacked with trash bags and junk. Yuri steps through the mess and politely knocks on an apartment door. After a long wait, Yuri can hear the bolt turning as the door is unlocked.

The door opens, and the bloodshot eye of an old woman peeks out. From behind the door, Pauline, a thin, frail woman draped in a ratty robe, stares at Yuri. She is visibly drunk, and alcohol fumes waft from the room.

"Yessss. Who is it?" Pauline asks.

Yuri tries to be as friendly as possible. "Hello. I'm a friend of your husband, Cosmo. And I—"

"Cosmo doesn't have any friends—at least none that are living. I don't know what you're selling, but we have no money." She tries to shut the door on Yuri.

"I'm not selling anything, I assure you. My name is Yuri, Yuri Yudin, and I—"

"Oh, I know who you are." And with that, she quietly closes the door, never looking up at Yuri. The bolt of the lock turns in the door with a sharp click.

Yuri is stunned, not sure what to do. He moves to knock again but stops. Quietly, he winds his way past the junk and leaves.

Outside the building, Yuri stands in the street. He sees the blurry figure of the man he wants to talk to, sitting near the window of the old apartment. Yuri watches the man for a moment, and then walks off into the night.

Three nights later, not far from the apartment Yuri had visited, the thumping of modern techno music emanates from a hot nightclub. The slick building is trimmed in stylish blue and purple neon and lights up the night. A line of nice cars moves along, dropping off well-dressed couples and groups of friends. Huge doormen and bouncers, with flashlights and walkie-talkies, organize the customers. Standing behind a velvet rope, fashionable women shiver in skimpy designer outfits.

Across the street from the loud club, Yuri sits on the curb, watching the party people. Next to him sits another homeless man, who rambles on about nothing Yuri cares about. Yuri watches as a delivery truck pulls past the front of the club and turns down the alley. The delivery truck is Yuri's cue, and he gets to his feet. His companion is insulted.

"Hey, where are you going? Were you even listening to me?"

"Nope, I was not," Yuri answers without even looking back. He crosses the street and follows the truck down the alley. He hangs back around the corner and uncovers a shopping cart that he'd stashed there the day before.

Yuri calmly peeks around the corner as the delivery truck parks and the fat driver climbs out. The back door of the club opens, and an older, sharply dressed bartender comes out, pushing a hand truck to help unload. The driver checks a clipboard, rolls up the gate of the truck and fills the hand truck with crates of bottled wine and spirits.

"How's it going tonight?" the bartender asks the driver.

"Uh…not too bad. I'm on time, and when I'm on time, I'm happy, the boss is happy, everyone is happy."

As the driver and the bartender load the crates, Yuri sneaks up and hides on the truck's blind side. From his cart, Yuri pulls a small glass bottle of petrol with a rag stuffed in it. He lights it and flings it in front of the truck. The fireball explodes.

The bartender spots it. From where he stands, it looks as if the truck is on fire. "Holy hell, buddy! I think your truck's on fire!"

The driver turns toward the bright orange glow of flames. "What the fuck? Get help!" The driver runs to the front of his truck while frantically dialing his phone.

The bartender turns and runs inside. "Fire! Fire," he shouts. "Get some more extinguishers! We got a truck on fire!"

Yuri quickly and precisely rolls his shopping cart up to the back of the delivery truck, drops three boxes of booze into it, throws a blanket over it, and wheels it out. Two more bartenders, with fire extinguishers, run around from the front of the building just as Yuri leaves the alley. They narrowly miss plowing into him as he walks away.

Two hours later, on the second floor landing of the bleak apartment building, Pauline and Cosmo can be heard arguing.

"Why can't we have proper food sometime?" Cosmo grumbles.

"You know as well as I, we don't have the money. And all that fatty, rich stuff is bad for your heart."

Pauline opens the door to set out a bag of trash but almost trips over a covered mound of boxes that blocks the doorway.

She is instantly furious and yells to the neighboring door, "Now you can't even take your own crap out? You're piling your garbage in front of my door, Mr. Ivanoff? You filthy dog! It's a fire hazard."

"Pauline, don't waste your breath. He's as deaf as post," Cosmo weakly calls from inside.

"I'm reporting you to the manager *again*, Victor Ivanoff!" she yells.

She scowls at the mound at her feet. She starts up again, screaming at the neighbor. "How am I supposed to get out of my own home without breaking my neck?"

She gives the covered mound a jab with her toe. The telltale tinkling of glass bottles clinking together changes her mood instantly. She delicately pulls back the blanket, revealing three boxes filled with fancy champagne, liquor and wine. She gasps.

"Holy cow, Cosmo!" She looks around suspiciously and then quickly drags in the alcohol and quietly closes the door. She pauses for a minute, takes out one bottle of wine, goes back out onto the landing, and leans it against the neighbor's door. She gently closes her door again.

From inside the apartment, ever so faintly, come the excited whispers and laughter of Cosmo and Pauline.

Yuri listens and smiles. He has hidden behind a pillar and some old furniture down at the dark end of the hall.

Three hours after the drinks have been served, Pauline staggers into the hall to bring out two empty champagne bottles. From Yuri's point of view, she's sufficiently drunk. Yuri finally stands up, cramped and sore. He stretches, takes off his hats, smooths his hair, and straightens himself, as if to be more presentable. Yuri starts to knock, but the door swings open.

Inside the tiny apartment, the free booze is set out on the table. The apartment is crowded and cramped, stuff piled on every surface. Pauline has passed out on an old couch, clutching a bottle. She wears a plastic New Year's Eve hat from 2002.

Across the room, Cosmo, the inspector, sits in his wheelchair. He is thin, and his skin is yellow and blotchy. His once-black hair is now gray and wispy.

Thick glasses balance on his nose as he sits close to a modest TV, watching the Weather Channel.

Yuri stands in the doorway. He doesn't want to startle the old man, so he gently knocks on the door frame and softly calls to Cosmo.

"Hello, sir?"

"Whoa! Yes, hello?" Cosmo is startled and turns to the door.

"I'm sorry. I went to knock, and it just opened." Yuri stands reverently outside the apartment.

"Oh, that's fine. My wife has had a bit too much to drink, I'm afraid. I think she forgot to latch it." Cosmo waves Yuri in.

"May I speak with you?"

Cosmo wheels over to Yuri. "I suppose. I've had a bit of this free liquor tonight, so you'll excuse me if I don't seem sharp as a tack."

"That's fine. I brought the liquor," Yuri confesses.

"You did? But why?"

"Well, I wanted to speak with you, but your wife wouldn't let me."

Cosmo studies Yuri's face intently and then smiles, He points at Yuri's face with his thin yellow finger. "You'd have been number ten," Cosmo quietly says.

"I would have," Yuri admits.

"I have some letters someplace—dozens of them actually—each with an elaborate theory as to the significance of the number nine in relation to your dead friends."

"Is that so?" Yuri says.

"Oh yes, I reviewed thousands and thousands of letters, but the ones that obsessed on the significance of the number nine were truly fascinating. One of them had a handwritten theory complete with charts and equations. It was easily 200 pages long with writing about this small." He demonstates with his fingers. "Tell me, where did you get all the liquor?"

"I stole it. I was hoping it would perhaps loosen your wife's grip on me seeing you."

"You've loosened it all right. Let's hope she doesn't lose her grip on her bladder. Hey, my darling bride!" Cosmo yells at Pauline who barely shifts. Cosmo continues to yell at his passed-out wife. "If you have to piss, get up, and get to the toilet! Do you hear me? PAU-LINE!!! You got that?"

Pauline is just conscious enough to be irritated. "Mmmhhhhhhhhhhaaaaaabbbb…"

She rolls over, and Cosmo explains it to Yuri. "What happens is, she'll piss on the couch, and then when she sobers up, wham! It's all my fault for not waking her!" He laughs to himself. He pours himself another glass of champagne.

"You want some of your illicit contraband?"

"I don't drink anymore, thanks."

"I remember you. I tailed you for weeks, and I talked to you in the dorm with your friend. And now you're here. After all this time, you found my name. You looked me up. Click, click, click on the computer. And now you want me to tell you what killed your friends."

Cosmo rolls into his study, a tiny closet, crammed with papers and files. He starts to look through things.

"I know who killed my friends," Yuri says, "but I want to know how I can prove it. And I want to know what they were testing. What was in the envelope? Why was it removed from any other official report?"

Cosmo, now 91 years old, has nothing to hide. "Tiny metal fragments. The envelope contained tiny metal fragments found at the campsite," Cosmo says.

"From what? What kind of metal? Radioactive? Something left over from their weapon?" Yuri asks. Finally, it seems he's getting some answers.

"What weapon? No, this was metal only because it looked like metal. But when tested, it wasn't metal, no metal anyone had ever seen before. The pieces were untestable, except that these fragments gave off radio waves so strong that if you held a portable radio even near them, it would make a strange static noise. No one had ever seen anything like it, and no one could explain it." Cosmo sips his champagne.

"Explain it? It was something they did. It was an effect of whatever they were testing," Yuri argues.

"Stop saying 'they!' There is no 'they,' I'm telling you. There were no tests. We knew nothing of what was up there."

"That's not true!" Yuri isn't swayed. "You had people up there. I was shooed away when I tried to return that spring, and I was followed—for years—afterwards. Nick and Rusty said they'd seen Dyatlov meeting with KGB all the time."

"Yes, the Kremlin wanted to know of the phenomena on that mountain. I found evidence of that. I was an investigator for the state. I was looking for any crimes, negligence, or criminal activity—by anyone. I found none."

Yuri is reeling. His theory of fifty years is starting to unravel. "You're lying. KGB sent us there. Dyatlov set us up—as guinea pigs. And you tested a weapon us, on them."

Cosmo dismisses the notion. "It is possible Dyatlov was sent there, but KGB knew very little. They knew something occurred on that mountain in some unknown cycle. I saw some documents at one point that suggested a cycle of activity, originally written years earlier by a geologist. They put it down as some sort of geothermal anomaly, although prior investigations were always inconclusive."

"No, no, no, this is too easy. You've got it all neatly packaged. It's the standard reflections-off-swamp-gas excuse. OK, maybe *you're* not lying, but they lied to you. And how can one hand not know what the other hand is doing? It's not possible. You're lying, and you don't even know it. It's been so long, and you've had so much time. You've convinced yourself it's the truth." Yuri starts to sweat. The apartment is stifling, and he takes off two of his coats.

Cosmo talks to Yuri calmly but frankly. "I can see what's happening. Your half-century conspiracy ideas are falling apart. Look around. Does it look as if I'm a part of any secret society? I'm a 91-year-old man. I investigated a strange phenomenon. That's it. I never figured it out. No one did. But I moved on to the rest of my career, my life. You on the other hand—"

"I...I...but I...I don't understand." Yuri slumps down in a kitchen chair.

Cosmo, with a surprisingly solid grip, holds Yuri's arm. "Welcome to the club, Yuri Yudin. You don't know how many people, how many men—doctors, engineers, top scientists—all joined the 'I don't understand' club that year."

Yuri talks, more to himself, than to Cosmo. "But the metal was from...the orange lights, the lights the other ski team, 100 kilometers due west, had seen that night. What they saw were rockets, the second-stage rockets coming back to earth. They...that metal...That metal proves that they created some sort of device, some sort of reaction—like the shell casing of a bullet."

Cosmo doesn't agree and waves it away. "No, no, no, no. No rockets. 1959 was the height of the cold war and the new space race. Everyone was keenly aware of who was launching what. And those little flakes of metal—33.35 grams of it—actually exonerates the Soviet government completely."

"What? But how?" Yuri asks.

Cosmo wags his finger at Yuri and strikes a serious tone. "Because the fragments found on the mountain were fragments identical to fragments found before the Soviet Union even existed."

"*Before?* I don't understand. No, they sold you a bill of goods. It's standard operating procedure!" Yuri's head is pounding.

Cosmo continues. "Sorry, Yuri. I saw the test results myself. Identical fragments were in the Russian archives already. Recovered back in 1910."

Yuri is flabbergasted. "1910? From the same area?"

"No, the early fragments were found in abundance—1,044 grams, if I remember correctly—from about 3,600 kilometers directly east, at Tunguska."

Yuri gets up and moves to the sink. Without asking, he picks up a cup, fills it with water, and guzzles it down. He sits back down.

"Tunguska? The blast?"

"Yes. Dug from a pit at the epicenter. They were collected in 1910 from the Tunguska blast site. It's the truth. Tunguska, one of the biggest releases of energy humans have ever known. A mystery. Look at me. Why would one very old man lie to another old man, really, at this point?"

Yuri actually feels dizzy and nauseous. "Tunguska?" Yuri mumbles.

"Why have you done this, Yuri Yudin? Why has this taken you over? One thing I am certain of, whatever killed your friends had to do with whatever those orange lights were. What those lights were, no one knows—except your friends. Do you somehow blame yourself? Is that it?"

"OK, OK, OK, I get it. I get it. It's fine. Thank you. I'm sorry. I'm sorry I wasted your time." Yuri gets up and fumbles with his coats and hats.

"You don't believe me, Yuri. Listen to me. There was nothing else like it. Yes, there was a time when KGB thought the Army was up to something. The Army thought the KGB was up to something. The Army and the KGB thought the scientists were up to something. In those days there was no communication, but then the heavies got involved, and it was all pulled together, and it turned out that no one knew anything at all."

Yuri goes back to the sink and wipes his face with water.

"I remember at one point," Cosmo continues, "several military men suggested a weapon from the West—perhaps Britain, France. They suggested that the U.S. launched or dropped something into the Urals that night, but that never held water. Like I said, we knew of every American launch days before the launch team was told."

"No, no, no, wait. Wait. Just stop. OK, I get it, I get it." Yuri is having a mild panic attack. "Thank you. I just need to think. I just…I just need to look at some… check some…look at some documents."

Cosmo tries to calm Yuri down. "Come, sit. Let's watch some TV. You want to watch TV? Do you like CSI? Let's watch CSI. Come on, have a drink."

131

Yuri refuses and heads toward the door. "No. No, thank you. I have to go."

Cosmo hands Yuri a bottle. Yuri considers it. He takes it, stuffs it into his pocket, and leaves.

Down on the street, Yuri walks away from the building, stunned. He looks at the bottle as he walks and finally cracks the lid. He takes a big swig and almost chokes. He's verging on hysteria. Yuri walks aimlessly through the night. His thoughts are a jumble.

Yuri shuffles in front of a busy fish-and-chips eatery. A group is leaving. One of the women carries a bag of leftovers.

"I'll give it to you, that was really pretty good," she says to her husband.

"See, it wasn't bad. They changed cooks, and it's really improved."

"Well, it's hard to ruin fish and chips," the other woman says.

The husband sees Yuri shuffling along in his daze.

"Hey, Karl Marx. You hungry? We didn't even touch these if you want them. I was just going to throw them out."

Yuri looks at the man. He looks almost like Alex fifty years ago. And now the woman looks almost like Zina. He closes his eyes—as if his eyes are playing tricks on him.

"Er...what?" Yuri asks.

"That came out wrong. They're fine. We didn't even touch them. Here." The woman hands Yuri the leftovers.

"Uh...OK, thank you. I...Do you know—"

"You're welcome." The group walks off.

Hours later, Yuri manages to find his way back

across town and finally home. In total darkness, navigating with his penlight, Yuri crawls through his hole-in-the-wall entrance. He sits down. His hands shake uncontrollably. He pulls out the bottle and takes a swig. He hasn't had a drink in years, and it burns his mouth and stomach. But it also softens his thoughts.

He lights his stove and sits, thinking and staring at his wall of clippings. After a long spell, his hunger pushes into his reeling mind, and he opens the bag of leftovers. He unwraps the cold fish and chips and slurps them down while he babbles and argues with himself.

"He's good. He's a good liar, and he almost fooled me, almost. They told him to say all that. It's too clean, too easy. Just too clean."

He unconsciously belches and is about to crumple up the newspaper that his fried fish came in when something catches his eye. He flattens the paper on the floor and pulls his lantern closer. He reads a small headline toward the bottom of the page: NATURAL GAS BURN-OFF OVER THE URALS TRIGGERS 'MYSTERIOUS' ORANGE LIGHTS.

Yuri can't read it fast enough. He finishes the page and flips it over looking for more, but the article is short. It briefly reports that the mysterious lights seen in the Urals are caused by a natural-gas pipeline burn-off. The hair on Yuri's neck stands on end, and fifty years of rage instantly boil over.

"Unbelievable! The bastards. They're doing it *again*. Goddamn it! They're at it again. Goddamn them. How many have to die?" In a frenzy, Yuri starts to pack his pack as he searches secret places around the derelict house for more cash. From behind boards, he takes out a small box. It yields only a few coins. He moves a rock in a broken wall, reaches in, and pulls out a tin can. He checks it—a few more coins. He checks other spots but knows he doesn't have enough money.

"You need some more goddamn money," he says to himself. Yuri finishes packing his pack and dashes out of his house and into the night.

It is dark and misty down by the thick Moskva River that winds through Moscow. Snow clings to the boats and barges moored in a huge industrial-dock area. Yuri walks out onto a dock. It's well past midnight, and he seems utterly alone.

A metal gate prohibits access to the rest of the dock. Yuri is surprisingly agile. He steps around the gate and, hanging out over the water, shimmies around the obstruction and back onto the other side of the dock. Silently he moves along the dock and creeps down the gangplank of a large river barge.

This barge is the home and business of Yuri's brother Franz and Franz's wife Celeste. Franz and Celeste quietly sleep in the small bedroom off the main cabin of the boat. The hypnotic sound of the water lapping at the hull is broken by an unfamiliar noise and Franz is immediately awake. In the darkness, he sits up and listens. He hears another noise. It's obvious that someone is trying to be quiet. His wife snores peacefully. He tries to wake her with a gentle shake, but she won't budge. She rolls over.

Quietly, Franz stands up and grabs a fishing club with a metal hook, kept for just such an occasion. He creeps into the main cabin. His heart leaps as he sees Yuri in the dark, hunched over, going through Celeste's purse. Franz snaps on the light.

"All right! Don't you move, asshole. I'll put this hook through your fucking head. Now—Yuri? Yuri? Goddamn it!"

Yuri stands, holding cash in one hand and Celeste's purse in the other. He offers a feeble excuse. "You...said I should come by."

"Oh, fuck you, Yuri! Damn it, you scared the shit out of me. You're going to give me a heart attack. I could have killed you. Celeste, she's in there, scared to death. And you're out here robbing me. Is that it?"

Yuri has been caught red-handed, and he can feel his face flush with embarrassment.

"I'm not...you know...robbing you. I...I just need a loan, enough for a train ticket."

Franz puts down the large club. He is furious. "Taking a trip? Where are you headed? Crazyland? Jupiter?"

"The mountain. They're at it again."

"Oooohhhhhh! Yuri, you're insane. You have been beating this drum for—what? Half a century? Half a fucking century? You know I could have you committed. You know that, right? And—Do I smell booze? You're drinking again? Yuri, what the hell?"

Yuri gets riled up, too. "Damn it, Franz! They're at it *again*. They're doing it again. Look! Look! Someone has to do something!" Yuri brandishes the greasy newspaper article.

Franz isn't moved. "Ummm...Yeah, this wouldn't be the first article you've chased. It's more—"

"Just *read* it!" Yuri yells.

Franz yells back. "I don't have to read it, Yuri." He hunts around and grabs his wallet from his pants in the other room.

"Here. Here. Here you go! Buy a goddamn train ticket. Get a meal, too. Go ahead. But make it a one-way ticket. I can't take this bullshit anymore. I have to get up and actually take this thing out onto the river and do some fucking work in—" he checks his watch "—six hours. So just go!"

"I'm sorry. I should have…But it's different this time. I know it. I can feel it. Franz, I can feel it. It's really—"

"Please, Yuri, for my sake, just go. Please go."

Yuri slinks toward the door of the boat. He tries to somehow acknowledge the favor, but Franz isn't interested.

"And if you come back here—like this again—I will put this hook in your head and put all of us out of our misery."

Yuri climbs out. Franz goes over to lock up. He examines the latch.

"Oh, and you broke the damn latch, asshole!" Celeste yells from the other room, "Will everyone please stop *yelling?*"

Yuri shakes off the guilt. He hurries to the subway and on to the train station.

It's again early morning, and almost no one is out and about. Yuri checks the schedule at a kiosk, buys a ticket, and heads through a turnstile to the track. He walks up the platform, alone except for a young man, who sits on a bench with a big backpack and skis listening to his headphones.

Yuri wanders over and sits down on the bench.

He takes a swig from his bottle. He offers the young man a sip.

The young man takes off his headphones and drinks from the bottle. "Thanks, mister. Thanks a lot. It's cold."

"No problem. You'd do the same for me." Yuri's words trail off as something seems strangely familiar about the moment.

"I would," the young man says.

"So where are you headed?" Yuri asks.

"Vizhai. Do you know how long it takes?"

Without warning, Yuri snatches his bottle from the boy's mouth. He runs around the corner, frightened and confused. He remembers his encounter from fifty years ago. Something is strange. He's felt all this before. He looks back, and the young man is gone from the bench. Yuri steps out and scans the platform. The young man is nowhere to be seen. Yuri is rattled. He sits back down, not sure what has just happened. He quakes with fear. For the first time, Yuri wonders if he is, in fact, losing his mind. For the first time, in half a century, Yuri begins to doubt his own sanity.

Over two hours, more early-morning travelers arrive at the platform. Eventually, the train pulls into the station. Yuri boards with the other passengers. He's confused and shaken and finds a lone seat that he drops into. He looks out the window, trying to clear his mind.

Still, for all his efforts, all he can see in his mind is the face of Lyudmila smiling and happy that day on the train platform—when she whispered in his ear. But as he begins to feel better, the image of the black-and-white photo of her autopsy pops into his head—her tortured face, torn and distorted. He shuts his eyes, and it's worse. So he simply gazes out the window, trying to control the thoughts that ravage his mind.

In the evening, the train stops in Vizhai, and Yuri is the only one to get off. A few workers and other waiting passengers board the train, and within a minute it is gone.

Yuri walks out expecting the menacing KGB agent to be there still, but there is no one. He breathes, and only the frozen vapor of his breath moves in the quiet night.

Yuri's plan hasn't gotten him any further than this. Snow falls steadily as he trudges into town. In darkness, he crunches through fresh snow. A loud garbage truck rumbles up the main street, turns, and is gone. The once-quaint village is much bigger. It's dotted with industrial buildings and dominated by some sort of plant or factory.

Yuri wanders around Vizhai, not sure what to do or where to go. He tries to remember his last good night's sleep, but he can't. All he knows is that he's exhausted and can't stop yawning. He sees a stairwell on the side of a small building and heads for it. He steps in and starts to take off his pack. Another homeless man is already in there.

"I don't know what you're thinking, pal, but this is a single-seater. Find your own hole."

"Oh…uh…Sorry. Any suggestions?"

From the darkness the man answers, "Hmmm. How about go fuck yourself and leave me alone."

"Thanks. You've been a big help."

Yuri shuffles off. A lone streetlight illuminates a tiny park, and Yuri spots a bench. He walks over and sweeps off the snow. He sits down, takes out his sleeping bag and blankets, and bundles up. He closes his eyes for a few seconds and then opens them. He looks straight ahead and is completely confused by what he sees.

He takes out his little flashlight and shines it on an ornate stone monument three meters tall behind a low iron fence. He staggers to his feet, staring at the polished stone block. Yuri cannot believe what he seeing. He is seated in front of a memorial to the Dyatlov dead, complete with photos etched in the stone, the names inscribed underneath each photo. He steps over the low fence and meticulously studies the images. There they are, as they were. Yuri recognizes the photos from their student-body cards. Their faces claw at his mind. He feels a lump in his throat as he lingers on the picture of Lyudmila.

Behind him, Yuri hears the crunching sounds of someone walking on the frozen snow. An old man shuffles out of the shadows. He speaks with a strange accent.

"Ah, Lyudmila, the girl. She met such a horrible fate." The tall man walks into the little park. He is very old and leans on a cane, but he still seems strong and sharp. "I knew you'd be back. I just didn't know if I'd still be here," he says, looking at Yuri.

"Wait a minute. You…You're…that Mansi tribesman we met. How did you know I'd be here?"

"I didn't know. I was just walking home. I live over there. And I drink over there." He points toward a trailer park and then toward a ratty bar. "But like I said, I knew we would meet again. But it's been a long time. Another ten years or so, and I would have started to get worried."

They look at each for a moment.

"It's strange how things work out like that," the old man continues. "I dreamt of your friends last night, but then I always dream of them. And that Dyatlov fel-

140

low."

"He wasn't my friend, I guess," Yuri mutters. "He got them all killed. Me, too, if I'd stayed. You...You're the chief."

"I *was* the chief. There's nothing to be chief of now. Come, let's get warm. Let's get out of the cold. Get away from that sad stone."

Surek and Yuri walk out of the park and down a dirt road. Trailers, abandoned cars and buses, heaps of trash and rusted metal mix in with little shacks, and even a few sod huts crowd the snowy field. Yuri follows Surek through the snowy debris into a large hut.

Surek's hut has a dirt floor, and yet there's a small TV sitting on a bench, with a soccer game blaring. Surek turns it off and stokes the fire in the middle of the dirt floor. Smoke wafts up and out of a hole in the wooden ceiling.

"You live alone here?" Yuri asks.

"Wife died in 1989. Cancer. Most of the tribe moved off to the Baltic to work on the gas lines. It's good money, and no one was buying reindeer anyway. It was just too hard to feed everyone. Half the land we used to cross is now fenced, and any time we settled, we were chased off by mineral or gas surveyors."

"Ahhh, the government. Real fair," Yuri mutters. Surek pours hot tea into a jar and hands it to Yuri. Yuri sips it.

"Fair is irrelevant," Surek continues. "There just isn't room for that kind of existence regardless of how much space you have. It's as if civilization has moved on. Plus, I love watching soccer and the dance shows. What shows do you watch?"

"I...don't have a favorite...or a TV," Yuri says. He tries to make small talk. "From what I gather, C.S.I.

is very popular…"

"Why are you here, Yuri?"

"You know why. They're up there at it again." Yuri roots through his pack and pulls out the newspaper clipping. "Look."

"You stay away, Yuri Yudin. But to look at you, you aren't going up there. You've got no gear. You've got no skis. You're old, tired, and drunk.

"I…I…I am—"

"Is this your plan? To run off in the middle of the night and chase down strange lights? Look at you. You'd have a stroke going up that mountain on a sunny day in spring. Are you going to take videos and put it on the TV for everyone to see?"

"I've got to see for myself what they're doing. I have to know. And don't worry about me. I'm fine outside. I can get around. I must know what they're doing. Someone needs to admit to what they've done."

"Yuri. It's not *they*. It's an *it*. Yuri, there are things in the universe that shouldn't mix with other things. Like the Americans mixing with the atom beat the Japanese into submission. But as Einstein says, 'Energy cannot be created or destroyed.' And that is how it should be. But there are things that so go against the order of things that they cannot be allowed to exist in this world. Instead they must be contained."

"What the hell are you talking about? Are you kidding me? This is the work of the KGB. It always has been, always will be," Yuri insists.

"KGB? Yuri, my people have lived in these mountains for thousands of years. The KGB couldn't find their own asses in a parking lot. Yes, they came here, but they knew nothing when they arrived and knew less when they left. This mountain has been the mountain of the dead for as long as anyone can remember."

Yuri breathes deeply and tries to contain his anger. "Oh, this magical, mystical crap. It's so colorful and convenient. I'm sorry. I think I should go."

Surek gazes into the fire. "You know, the night your friends were on the mountain, I had the most horrific dream—perhaps the scariest dream of my entire life. I gathered our men, and we tried to make it up the mountain. But the storm was too strong. It was a two-day hike, and we—I'm sorry, Yuri. Maybe if we had tried harder, forged ahead."

Yuri's mind is slipping. His convictions are slipping. He says the words, but he can feel their meaning and their determination crumbling away. "I can't really, and...and you're right. I need gear. I do need skis—or one of those snowmobile machines. Are any of those around here? I'll...I'll go and...I'll..." Yuri gathers up his bag and coats.

Surek watches the fire but speaks softly to Yuri. "Yuri, are you sure I can't talk you out of it? Come, stay the night. You can go out first thing in the morning. It's only a few hours to dawn."

"No, thank you. You've been very kind. I need to press on. I'm not tired. I—"

Surek strokes the fire. "You need to sleep, Yuri Yudin. You need to sleep."

Surek throws a handful of dust into the fire. The little particles burn briefly, swirling in the flames and darting out of the hole in the ceiling.

Yuri shakes his head and is suddenly overcome with dizziness. He rubs his forehead and staggers. "Oh, I think it's too smoky in here. I need to get some air."

Yuri stands weakly and tries to walk to the entrance of the low hut. He passes out, crumpling to the floor.

Yuri awakens into darkness. It is night. A storm blows with a raging force outside. The tent walls flap and whip against the howling wind. The air is bitterly cold and smells stale. Ice crystals have formed on his scraggly beard around his nose and mouth.

Yuri is confused. "Is this Surek's tent? How did I get here?" He tries to remember what happened, and the harder he tries to pin down the memories, the more quickly they vanish. He sits up and looks around. His throat closes, and he is paralyzed with fear when he realizes where he is. It must be a dream, a nightmare. Yuri's mind screams, "It's surely a horrible nightmare."

As his eyes adjust in the dim light, Yuri knows he is in the tent just as it all is about to begin. Confused, he looks around. In front of him, Lyudmila sleeps. He can't believe he is seeing her again, still so young and beautiful after so many years. It is a dream, he is convinced, but at this moment, he is grateful to be in it. His emotions swing wildly, and his eyes brim with tears. Yuri takes off his ratty glove and is about to touch Lyudmila's cheek, but he stops short when he sees his own aged and wrinkled hand hovering over her youthful skin. If it is a dream, he wants it to continue, just like this—forever—so he can simply gaze at her alive and blissfully asleep.

He whispers to her. "Lyudmila, Lyudy. I can't believe it. It's me. It's me, Yuri."

Yuri's eyes have adjusted to the dim light, and he can see now. The whole team is sacked out in the tent as the storm roars outside. Alex, Lexy, Lyudmila, and Nick still wear their ski suits as they sleep.

Yuri strokes Lyudmila's hair. She stirs and turns over, and Yuri spots the compass he gave her, around her neck. His mind doesn't know how to process what he's seeing. It's too real, but it must be a dream. Suddenly the needle on the tiny compass starts to move slowly. It turns, makes a lazy revolution, and then simply goes berserk, spinning around madly, flipping back and forth.

Yuri realizes what's about to happen.

"Oh, no! No, no, no! This…This isn't real! It… It's—Lyudmila! Lyudmila! Wake up! You've got to wake up! I've got to wake up! I—Doroshenko! Alex! Alex!"

Yuri can't wake anyone, no matter how loud he screams or how forcefully he prods them.

Outside, in the swirling blackness of the storm, fifty meters from the tent, a noise like no other explodes into the night. The ground trembles and buckles. Beyond the tent, a massive rock outcropping crowns the slope. With a flash, a short arc of lightning rips from the ground striking the rock again and again. Blackness seeps out of the rock, and the orange lightning coils into explosive balls in the sky.

In the swirling, whipping snow, something huge emerges from the rock. It reflects no light, but

snowflakes slap against it and stick before quickly melting. The pelting snow defines the amorphous outline
of a massive being. The orange lightning briefly arcs
and snaps from the rock, throwing the massive, moving shape into silhouette as it forms from the ground.
Distorted human figures and forms arc and snap in the
orange lightning.

Inside the tent, Yuri huddles against a tent wall.
Now wide awake, they are all, like Yuri, paralyzed with
fear. They stare transfixed at Dyatlov, in his long underwear, standing at the front of the tent. He jerks spas-
modically and babbles gutturally in other languages and
voices.

Alex finally calls out to him. "Dyatlov! Dyatlov!
What's wrong? What's happening?"

"Dear God!" Zina screams. "Dyatlov! What's
wrong?"

Dyatlov's body is rigid. Suddenly he begins to
float off the tent floor.

The others leap to their feet when an explosive
orange light engulfs the front of the tent.

Doroshenko screams above the deafening
sounds. "Zina! Georgi! We've got to get out of here!"

Dyatlov hangs in the air, screaming and sobbing.
"I'm sorry. I'm so sorry. I didn't know. I didn't know.
Please, please forgive me… Please go! You've got to get
out of here! Go!"

During the brief, intense flashes, the team can
see shapes—distorted human figures, shadows—pro-
jected on the tent wall, forming in the blinding light.
Dyatlov stands transfixed as the others cower away.
Another burst of energy slaps Dyatlov to the ground,
knocking him unconscious. The lightning has sub-
stance. Twisted human hands push on the fabric of the

tent. Heads, spines, mangled faces and limbs stretch the glowing tent canvas. The force pushes against the tent like thick liquid, shafts of orange light punch through ragged holes in the worn canvas. The noise is excruciating. Howls, voices, cries, guttural sounds, all wail thickly. The students try to scream over the cacophony.

"Rusty, what is it?" Zina screams.

"I don't know, but we can't stay here," Rusty yells.

A few cover their ears and seal their eyes shut. They cower on the opposite side of the tent. It seems that the force—whatever it is—is deliberately tormenting them.

Doroshenko yells, "Move back!" He takes his knife and carves into the back wall of the tent. He cuts a large hole, and he and Georgi leap out. He tosses the knife to Rusty, who carves away at the tent as well.

"Everyone out! Get out of the tent and run!" Doroshenko screams.

No one needs further encouragement as they all bolt from the undulating tent.

Zina and Rusty drag out an unconscious Dyatlov.

The snow is waist deep, but they run with all their energy. The tattered tent whips and flaps against its fraying ropes. In front of the tent, the force moves as it changes form. Alex looks back as he runs, trying to get a clear view of whatever it is, but with every flash it seems to be a different shape and size.

Everybody runs in different directions. Doroshenko and Georgi blindly run down the hill away from the camp. Behind them the mountain flashes with orange light. The thundering noises swirl and echo though the valley. They can hear shouts from the camp, but Georgi and Doroshenko keep running. They crash into

148

the trees and slide under a huge pine tree, out of breath and terrified. Georgi almost runs past Doroshenko, but Doroshenko pulls him in and tries to calm him. They are both terrified and babble incoherently.

All at once, the attack stops, and the deafening noise and energy vanish, leaving only the howling storm.

Georgi claws at Doroshenko. "I can't see. I can barely see. It was so bright. Good God, what was that? What in the hell was that?"

Doroshenko rubs his eyes and shakes his head. "I can't see right either. It was so bright. I...I saw bodies. I saw faces against the tent. It was like a dream."

Both are in only their underwear.

Georgi mumbles to himself, "I think I'm dreaming. Was it a demon? Was it Satan?"

"I don't know," Doroshenko mumbles. "It was alive."

Georgi's teeth chatter as he tries to speak. "Do you think the others are OK?"

Doroshenko hops around, trying to keep moving. "We're going to freeze as soon as this adrenaline dies down. We're going to freeze to death. We've got to build a fire. We've got to build a fire now."

"OK, OK. But I can't go up there. I just can't. I don't know what that was. And what if it returns?" Georgi moans.

Doroshenko kicks into survival mode. "Stand up. Move around, Georgi. Break off some branches for a fire. Climb up. See if you can see anything."

Georgi is still in a daze. "Was it Satan? Did you see bodies? I saw bodies. And they were alive. It was so bright. Maybe...I'm dreaming?"

Doroshenko sweeps together twigs and pine

needles. "I saw bodies, too. I saw bodies. I thought that they…I thought that they…saw me, too. I don't think we're dreaming. I've never been so cold in a dream." Doroshenko takes a box of matches from his sock and starts to work.

"I…It's hard to see. I can't see right," Georgi says.

Doroshenko lights a pile of twigs and needles. They crackle and burn. He feeds more tiny sticks into the flames.

"Rub your feet. Rub your hands," Doroshenko commands. "You'll get frostbite. Stand on the stump, not in the snow. Don't fall asleep. Do not fall asleep! You're starting to get hypothermia, Georgi."

"What *was* that? What does it want?" Georgi is lost in his own fears.

"Georgi, are you listening to me? Doroshenko barks. "Georgi, do what I say, or you'll die!"

Several hundred meters away, Zina and Rusty are carrying Dyatlov down the mountain, also heading away from the camp.

Zina has some of her winter clothing on. She gasps for breath. "It's some electrical force, some sort of lightning or something. It's affected our reasoning. It affected my thoughts. It's like some mass hypnosis or something. We have to stop for a minute. He's too heavy."

"Uhhhhhhh…I'm sorry. I'm so sorry." Dyatlov comes to, moaning and babbling.

"Just take it easy, Dyatlov," Rusty says. "We're going to get us all out of here. Which way did the rest go?"

"I don't know," Zina says. "I didn't see anyone except that…thing."

A few dozen meters away, Lyudmila, Nick, Alex, and Lexy climb out from the deep snow, where they've hidden. They are unharmed. They button up their warm clothes. Whatever happened now seems over, and the howling night has returned to normal.

Nick flips on his flashlight. He breathes rapidly. "What could that have been? What was that?"

Lexy sits in the snow. He, too, is badly shaken. "It was dead. It made me feel dead to see it. I felt as if I were dying. I've never felt so suddenly sick"

"It's…It's… a being or a…I don't know. I need to think," Nick mutters.

Lyudmila is scared and yet pragmatic. "We can't sit here. We've got to get back and get the others," she says.

Slowly they gather themselves together and slog through the blowing snow, back up the hill and back to the camp. The ransacked site crackles with a strange energy. Nick finds another flashlight and turns it on.

"This light works, Lyudmila," he says. "Help me put it up on that pole. Maybe the others will see it and come back."

Yuri, too, has hidden in the snow. He follows them back to camp. He haunts them. He knows they cannot hear them, but he babbles on.

"No, you can't stay here. It's not through. It's just toying with you. Please go on down the hill. Get to the trees. Just get out of here," Yuri begs.

Lyudmila starts to sob as the others try to figure out what has happened.

Further down the hill, at the tree line, Georgi and Doroshenko still huddle under the large tree, fumbling around and pulling down wet branches as they shiver uncontrollably. They scrape together twigs to feed their pitiful fire, but it's still too small.

Georgi is worried about the fire. "The fire, the

fire!" he cries. "What if that...What if it doesn't like fire? We...I..."

Doroshenko is more lucid than Georgi as he tries to get more twigs into the fire. "Georgi, listen to me," he says. "We have to get warm, and then we have to go back and get our clothes and food. We'll die if we don't."

Georgi recoils from the idea, manically shaking his head. "No, no, no. I don't care. I don't care if I die. I'm not going back up there. I can't...I...just...I...can't."

Between Georgi and Doroshenko and the original camp, Zina and Rusty, carrying Dyatlov, see the tiny fire in the darkness.

Zina points. "Look, a fire! That might be Alex! C'mon, we can make that. Call to them. Maybe they can help us with Dyatlov."

Rusty weakly calls out into the storm. "Alex! Nick! Come quick! Dyatlov is hurt! Georgi?"

Down at the fire, Doroshenko is shaking uncontrollably as he strips green needles off a branch. He struggles to see and can't stop wiping his eyes. He pauses and listens.

"I think I heard something. Someone is calling to us. Georgi, go up that tree and see what you can see."

Georgi is fading fast. He's small and skinny and almost naked. He sits rolled in a ball, shivering by the tiny fire. On Doroshenko's orders, he pulls himself up and tries to climb into the tree, but he's too cold. He falls down.

Doroshenko doesn't notice Georgi crumple to the ground, as he mindlessly rips at twigs. He's peers out into the night and spots the flashlight back at camp.

"Georgi! I can see a light! I think it's a flashlight at the camp. I think it's the 'all clear!' We can go back up.

We…we…just need to warm up. Georgi, stand up. Keep your circulation going. One of us has to get our clothes."

Doroshenko has stopped shivering. He starts to yawn and can't stop. "We need to warm up, get warm. I think it's working. I can feel the fire. It's good. It's working. I'm going to rest, Georgi. Georgi, Georgi, can you go up there for me and get my…my hat?"

Georgi, slumped over in a tight ball, is dead.

Doroshenko, delirious, doesn't notice. He talks and works on the twigs for a few more minutes. He sits down, looks up, and listens to night. "I can hear music, Georgi. I can hear music." Doroshenko dies.

Just beyond the bodies of Georgi and Doroshenko, Zina and Rusty drag Dyatlov toward the tiny fire. They struggle through the snow. Finally they slide into the base of the large tree. The snow they push snuffs out the fire with a tiny puff of steam.

"Oh, no. They're dead, Georgi and Doroshenko. They're both dead." Zina trembles and shivers. "What are we going to do? Rusty, what are we going to do? Do you have matches? Let's get this fire going again. We can burn their clothes to get it going. One of these two must have matches. Help me look, Rusty."

Rusty, too, is now delirious as hypothermia sets in. He spots the flashlight at the camp and snaps to. "Zina, look up there. It's a light at the camp. We have to go back. We can get the rest of our clothes, set up another tent." Rusty grabs a scarf and a hat from the bodies, the only winter clothing Georgi and Doroshenko wear.

"We've got to try and go back," says Rusty.

Dyatlov drifts in and out of consciousness. In a lucid moment, he speaks. "Leave me. Go on. I'm so sorry. I'm so sorry. I never knew. I didn't know what they meant. I would have never…I would never have brought you all up here. Take my clothes. Please go!"

Rusty and Zina look at each other and begrudgingly oblige. Zina undresses Dyatlov.

"What did you mean? Why did you bring us here?" Rusty demands.

Dyatlov is fading fast. "I was helping…I was helping…trying to help them, but they said they just wanted me to take pictures and take some notes. I didn't know…"

Zina slips on Dyatlov's gloves. "I think he means the KGB."

"I know who he means. C'mon, we've got to go." Rusty starts to yawn and slur his words.

Dyatlov cries, and his tears instantly freeze on his face. "I'm sorry. Tell the others I'm sorry. I'll…I'm…"

Drunken with cold, Rusty bursts into laughter. "Are you kidding? You fucking worm! You tried to impress your party friends—and now look at us. We're going to die. It's so—you."

Rusty laughs harder. Zina tries to drag him along, but he resists. He's now delirious with hypothermia. "You know what? I'm fine, really," he says as he lies back in the snow. "It's not even that cold, but I am tired. How're you doing, Igor Dyatlov, famous Soviet spy?"

Next to Rusty, his head slumped over in a snow bank, Dyatlov is dead.

"See. He dozed off," Rusty giggles.

Zina fights to keep moving. She talks to Rusty. "Rusty, I'm taking your scarf and Dyatlov's. I'm sorry. You're going to die, and I want to make a try of it."

"Go ahead. I told you. I'm not even that cold. I'm warm, even. I thought of something."

"What? What did you think of?" Zina puts

Rusty's hat on and wraps his scarf around her face.

Rusty slurs his speech as he tries to talk. "What we need is some chocolate syrup, and then we could have—ice cream! Iiiiccceee cream. I love ice cream."

Zina just slogs away without responding.

Rusty elbows Dyatlov's body. "What do you think? Ice cream, Dyatlov? I'm going to go back, and… uh…get some chocolate soup. So I'm going to go do that." Rusty stands up, takes a few slow steps, and sits back down. He giggles once more and closes his eyes. He's dead.

Zina trudges up toward the camp, but she's out of energy. She flops into the snow, panting and gasping for breath. She tries to stand again, but she is too tired and dizzy. She sits down, her panting stops, and she silently dies.

On top of the slope, at the camp, Nick, Lexy, Alex, and Lyudmila pace around, not sure what to do. Yuri stands away from the four, terrified and confused. The four team members have bundled up. Lexy gathers trampled supplies out of the snow. Lyudmila calls into the night for the others. Lexy and Nick assemble boots, gloves, and ski equipment.

"What are we waiting for? Let's get the fuck out of here. I want to be out of this place," says Lexy.

Nick shouts a few more times for the others. "We can't leave without the others. We can't!" he says.

Lyudmila calls into the storm. "Rusty! Georgi! Come back! Zina, Zina! Can you hear me? Dyatlov, Dyatlov! Can anyone hear me?" Lyudmila yells.

Alex holds up an empty ski coat. "They don't have winter clothes. If they haven't kept moving, then they're already dead."

Yuri is at the point of breaking. He stands

clutching his head. He mumbles to himself. "This isn't real. This is *not* real. Lyudmila, I'm sorry. I'm sorry I didn't stop you. I'm sorry I didn't take you back with me. I'm so sorry."

Suddenly, the sickening orange lightning begins to flash above them as the noise grows. The tall form materializes in front of them. Nick, a ski pole in his hand, instinctively flings it into the energy. The pole explodes into blinding sparks.

"Go! Go! Run!" Alex cries.

The team breaks from the camp again and runs back down the hill. The force seems to swirl and churn as it slowly follows them. Fearing that the entity will overtake him, Yuri ducks down into a large indentation in the snow. He is flat on his back as it passes just to his left. The wail of this thing—its noise and its energy— rattles Yuri's mind as he struggles to breathe. He's never had a dream like this.

The group runs nearly a half-mile. Once the being has moved past him, Yuri rises and slowly follows them, slogging through the snow as best he can.

At the ridge, Lyudmila gasps for breath. "Uh... uh...I have to stop. I...can't..."

Alex tries to scoop her up and keep going. "We've...we've got to keep moving. It's coming. It's still coming."

"It's gaining on us," Lexy gasps.

Nick, also out of breath, tries to glance back, but he's too scared as they plow through the deep snow. "I just want to wake up, I just want to wake up," he pants.

The four continue for another exhausting stretch across the snow-filled valley until they are forced to stop at the edge of a precipice. A frozen stream lies ten meters below. Alex almost steps over in the faint light.

"Whoa!" Nick grabs his shoulder and pulls him back.

"This way!" Lexy follows the edge of the cliff into more trees.

"We need a place to hide, a cave or something," says Alex.

They try to go around, but they discover they are caught on the outcropping.

The entity is moving toward them, howling and almost laughing.

The group turns back and hides in a grove of trees.

Yuri slogs behind, watching, trying to catch up. Yuri has lost track of them in the storm. He frantically searches for Lyudmila.

Suddenly, Lyudmila walks up to Yuri and stands in front of him. She glides along, and, to Yuri's amazement, she doesn't disturb the snow. Yuri stands with Lyudmila. He can hear the creature moving away, chasing down the rest of the team. Lyudmila is calm and beautiful and wears a simple dress, a spring dress. Her hair, in two long braids, is wound on her head. She's obviously not cold and seems completely at peace. Lyudmila grasps Yuri's hand gently. Her skin is warm and soft. She motions toward where the team desperately runs from the being.

"I'm going to die over there now, Yuri. But it's not in vain because we held it and bought them precious time. If it had escaped the mountain before they arrived, it could have been—much worse. But we kept it here. We kept it where it belongs. They're coming now, Yuri. " She trails off and looks skyward. "Now they're coming."

Yuri's brain struggles with the reality around

him.

"Lyudmila, I—"

"Good-bye, Yuri."

"Lyudy, I…I'm sorry I didn't take you with me that day. I…should have…I…"

She touches his face.

"Why did you spend so much of your life wondering about the last seconds of mine?"

"I…I didn't want you to have died for…I thought—"

Lyudmila takes the tiny compass from around her neck and presses it into Yuri's hand. "Here. I want you to have this. I don't need it anymore. Good-bye, Yuri Yudin."

A swirl of snow blinds Yuri for a moment. He closes his eyes and shields his face from the pelting snow. When he opens his eyes, Lyudmila is gone.

In the distance, Yuri sees the creature is closing in on the remaining four at the edge of the precipice. To Yuri's horror, Lyudmila is back among the terrified skiers, running for their lives. Yuri runs toward them, screaming and calling to them. Helplessly, he watches as the creature corners Nick. With snapping and arcing energy, it picks Nick up. He screams and thrashes.

Thick protrusions from the changing force act almost like huge, powerful arms that slam together and crush Nick's skull. His body slumps, instantly lifeless. The others watch helplessly as Nick, now drenched in steaming blood, drops into the snow.

Yuri falls to his knees, clutching his eyes and sobbing.

Alex and Lexy try to run from the spot, but the formless black shape throws a blow that flashes with a glowing blast that crushes Lexy's chest, knocking him back several meters.

Alex drops and begs for mercy but is swatted twenty meters into the air. Alex tumbles end over end through the snow and lies twisted and dead.

Yuri can't bring himself to look until he hears the angry screaming of Lyudmila. Everyone else is dead, but Lyudmila is defiant to the end.

"Come on, you miserable ass!"

The creature looks at her with curiosity. For the moment, it seems almost amused.

"Damn you! Damn you to hell, you filthy pig! Who do you think you are, you worthless dog? You're nothing. You're a worthless piece of shit!"

The creature stands before her and mimics what she's said, repeats it, in a strange screeching distortion, over and over. Then, without warning, a blow smashes into her chest. She flies through the air and hits a huge tree, dying instantly.

Yuri silently sobs. He pulls himself into a ball. His brain seems as if it will boil in his skull. Still, Yuri has to see. He peeks up from where he lies. He watches the creature toy with Lyudmila's dead body, seeming to scream at her with hundreds of strained, warped voices and sounds. The sounds soften into hissing whispers as the force quiets and huddles over her body. Yuri can only glimpse the creature from his hiding place.

All is silent, except for the zapping and crackling of energy that surrounds the creature. It is curious about the bodies and plays with them, shaking them, as if trying to see if it can squeeze out any more life. Eventually, it lines them up neatly at the bottom of the ravine.

Yuri's anguish is complete. He sobs on his knees.

Suddenly, the force seems to listen. It sniffs the air. It is now aware of Yuri and starts to move through the snow. Yuri tries to slog away, but it's no use, his energy is spent, he has nothing left. It's coming at him quickly. The creature is almost on top of Yuri, just a few meters away, when it senses something and stops. Yuri, struggling with his sanity, sees that the creature, like Lyudmila, moves without disturbing the snow.

Suddenly, it is quiet. The wind ceases. The clouds above the meadow glow with an orange light. Then, high above the meadow, several orange spheres silently drop from the thick clouds. The creature screams and rages in anger. Yuri looks up, his mouth hanging open, as he stares at the orbs. They look like glass spheres, several meters across, with a glowing orange energy that churns inside. The spheres make no noise and fly effortlessly in every direction.

On the ground, in the snow, the creature is enraged. It pounds the ground and writhes in anger. The orbs silently move into formation, and a flash bursts from the sky. A warp of energy moves over the landscape, and with a crackle, the screaming creature writhes and melts back into the ground.

The forest is deathly quiet as the spheres rise up and vanish into the thick cloud cover. Yuri shivers in the cold. He's fighting to maintain consciousness. It's all beyond anything he could ever have imagined, and he grapples with his emotions as little bits of energy still crackle in the snow. He only wants to wake from this horrible nightmare.

The anguish of seeing Lyudmila killed, his being on the mountain fifty years earlier, it is all too much. He doesn't cry any more. He is done. Yuri Yudin is resigned to simply stand where he is and die.

A meter away, a shadow appears on the snow and catches his eye. Initially, it's a tiny stain, but it begins to grow. It becomes a hand-sized depression in the snow. Yuri realizes what is happening. The snow is melting from underneath. Steam starts to rise as the snow melts more rapidly. Yuri snaps to and moves back. The snow melts around him. Within seconds, he stands on wet, muddy ground in the middle of waist-deep snow. The spot grows and steams. Yuri moves away, just as the ground starts to twitch and shudder.

The ground cracks open, and the cracks run out under Yuri's feet. Yuri tries to jump back, but he falls, as the ground lurches and buckles in unearthly hitches. Light and energy stream out of the pulsing cracks as acrid smoke and flames shoot up. Yuri can't move. He slips and slides on the bucking ground. He's surrounded by flames. Reflexively, Yuri covers his face as he's enveloped by fire.

Yuri awakens in a thick cloud of smoke. He is on the floor of his derelict house in Moscow. The wall, the ceiling, and most of the floor leap with huge flames. Yuri gasps and chokes for air. He's disoriented and staggers around the room He glances at his wall of clippings, now completely engulfed in fire as burning pages flutter through the thick smoke. He swipes at a burning clipping that lands on his shoulder. His normal exit is blocked as burning debris rains down. Hacking and coughing, he finally moves some old furniture and falls through a cardboard-covered window into the snow outside.

The three-story building is fully engulfed, and huge flames leap off the roof and push thick smoke into the night sky. Yuri gasps for breath and chokes. He grabs a handful of snow and stuffs it into his mouth. He rolls over, spits, and sits up. He hacks and coughs and finally draws a few breaths of cold night air. Yuri opens his hand. He stares, dumbfounded, at the tiny compass sitting in his palm.

From across an alley, a couple of other homeless

men emerge to investigate.

"What happened?" a man asks.

"Hey, are you OK? Is that your place?" another man asks.

Yuri cannot believe what he is seeing.

One of the men prods Yuri. "Hey, are you OK? Hey, papa. Hey, papa! Hey, mister! Hello?"

"Yes, it was my place." Yuri is fixed on his hand.

"Well, is there anyone else in there?"

"No. Just me. I…I…I must have kicked over my…my lantern while I was sleeping."

In the distance, the wail of fire engines can be heard.

One of the men helps Yuri to his feet. "You'd better go mister," he says. "They're going to want to talk to you." The two homeless men get Yuri to his feet.

Yuri shows the man the compass. "Do you see this?" Yuri asks.

"What?"

"Can you see this?" Yuri demands.

The homeless fellow is a little confused. "Yep, I see it. A compass. And if I were you, papa, I'd use it and go—" the man studies the compass "—sort of north northeast, pretty damn quick."

The two men hustle Yuri along. One wipes his face with snow, trying to wake him more thoroughly.

"Go that way, through the housing projects. And go down into the metro. Walk on pavement because they might follow your tracks. Go. Go!" They give him a good shove in the right direction, and he shuffles off in a daze, his gaze fixed on the tiny compass in his hand.

The next morning, by the river, Yuri walks down the ramp toward his brother's barge. The sun is coming up. The dock bustles with activity as gulls squawk overhead. Yuri walks down the gangplank between the boats. He stops. He takes the compass from his pocket and examines it. He flips it over. He squints at the tiny writing. He'd forgotten that he had it engraved. He reads it as tears distort his vision, "*To Lyudmila, May you always find your way. Yuri.*"

A young boy and his sister, obviously boat residents, come up the dock carrying school books and backpacks. The girl rushes past Yuri, but the boy stops. He's noticed Yuri staring into his own hand.

The curious boy walks up to Yuri and sees the small compass. Yuri and the boy exchange glances. Yuri gives the boy a look that says, "You want this?" The boy, without saying a word, smiles and sticks out his hand. Yuri drops the compass into the boy's hand. The boy smiles and runs off the dock and into town.

Yuri turns and walks down the dock toward the boats as the sun rises over the water.

Mike Wellins is a writer, film maker, visual artist, oddities museum owner, and has authored several books. Among his titles are *Stella's Babysitting Service*, *Serious Wackos*, and a textbook; *Storytelling Through Animation*. He has always had an interest in mysteries and odd phenomena. Mike resides happily in rainy Portland, Oregon with his terrier Leonard.

www.freakybuttrue.com

20704844R00090

Made in the USA
Lexington, KY
17 February 2013